COMMANDER *of the* RIVER

GLOBAL AFRICAN VOICES

Dominic Thomas, editor

COMMANDER *of the* RIVER

UBAH CRISTINA ALI FARAH

translated by Hope Campbell Gustafson

INDIANA UNIVERSITY PRESS

This book is a publication of

Indiana University Press
Office of Scholarly Publishing
Herman B Wells Library 350
1320 East 10th Street
Bloomington, Indiana 47405 USA

iupress.org

 The paper used in this publication meets the minimum requirements of the American National Standard for Information Sciences—Permanence of Paper for Printed Library Materials, ANSI Z39.48-1992.

Manufactured in the United States of America

Originally published as *Il Comandante del Fiume*

First Printing 2023

Cataloging information is available from the Library of Congress.

ISBN 978-0-253-06549-0 (hdbk.)
ISBN 978-0-253-06550-6 (pbk.)
ISBN 978-0-253-06551-3 (web PDF)

A Note on the Translation

UBAH CRISTINA ALI FARAH is considered one the most powerful, talented, and accomplished voices in Italian contemporary letters. Following *Little Mother* (2011), *Commander of the River* will be her second novel to be published in the Global African Voices Series. The translation is the outgrowth of a long-standing collaboration between the author and translator Hope Campbell Gustafson that began at the University of Iowa in the translation workshop, continued during a residency at the Art Omi Translation Lab, and resulted in a PEN/Heim grant. I also had the opportunity to work closely with Ubah Cristina Ali Farah at the *Italy and the Geopolitics of Migration: Aesthetic Approaches Conference* held at the University of California, Los Angeles, in October 2018 and later at the Alpen Fellowship Annual Symposium in Fjällnäs, Sweden, in 2019, where the work was presented and discussed.

Many of the authors previously published in the series have received extensive critical attention precisely because of their innovative and pioneering use of language and their capacity for, and determination to, experiment. Every translation, by definition, introduces linguistic challenges. Much like the River Tiber that twists through ancient Rome and opens onto the contemporary global capital, the Afro-Italian youth in the novel, as Italian scholar Alessandra Di Maio has argued, "chart their own paths forward as they confront the same issues faced by all Afro-descendants in the world." Readers will also be able to join this enthralling journey as they navigate Ubah Cristina Ali Farah's transformative text and open their imagination onto new landscapes.

The novel can set one off-compass because of the unorthodox punctuation and typography. This is a not a feature that is unique to the translation. Indeed, the skill of the translator stems from the ability to reckon with the full linguistic spectrum ranging from teenager jargon to a more reflective, lyrical style. Dialogues read in English as easily as they do in Italian, and the narrating rhythm is well preserved, as is the narrator's stream of consciousness. Hope Campbell Gustafson has identified and respected the nuances of the Somali language and storytelling, as well as the original goals and intentions of the author, and maintained various expressions while adhering to deliberate variations in content and form. These were to be found in the original Italian and in the dynamic process through which that language is expanded, enriched, augmented, and ultimately "decolonized" and revitalized as it is stretched in new and often unanticipated directions.

Commander of the River is a postmodern, postcolonial novel that reveals Italy's multicultural face, a timely work as the country struggles to reconcile its remarkable diversity with the disquieting rhetoric of far-right political parties who embrace an outdated vision of national identity and belonging. In many ways, the language and syntax, much like the world of the protagonists, are not linear, and Ubah Cristina Ali Farah's novel reflects the dismembered and fractured state of politics today.

In discussing Ubah Cristina Ali Farah's work, Hope Campbell Gustafson has repeatedly emphasized how the boundaries of Italian are pushed, but so too are the boundaries in English. This means that seemingly "foreign" terms are to be found in the novel, but the author and translator trust the reader to interpret and remember these, to enlist them in the process of enhancing their understanding but also of being comfortable with the various silences. Readers will encounter a number of unusual stylistic choices, but these are deliberate, and the translation has adeptly respected these as intrinsic elements of the work's pacing and traditions of spoken language. For Hope Campbell Gustafson, the aim has been to seamlessly weave Somali words and phrases into the narration, often without glosses and translations that could produce an alienating effect on English readers, and therefore highlight forms of linguistic resistance that pave the way for an alternative "soundscape" of sorts. These choices reflect a desire to create, combine, and recombine words, since as Sony Labou Tansi famously stated, "You can't make an omelet without breaking the words!"

Dominic Thomas, Editor

COMMANDER *of the* RIVER

IF YOU THINK I'm about to confess that it's all my fault, think again. People get all kinds of ideas when they see me—about where I'm from, who my parents are, where I live, whether I'm doing well in school. You know, a nice little prepackaged picture. But let me tell you, you can't expect to understand someone's story at first sight—you've got to arm yourself with patience and listen, to realize, for one, that it's our choices that show what we're made of. Like when there are religious icons at the corners of intersections, right where paths split. Some people leave them flowers or candles. Even though I'd never think of doing something so strange, I know those little Madonnas and saints hold a special meaning for many. They're there to remind travelers that they're always running the risk of making a wrong turn.

Well, that's not a mistake I ever want to make. I've spent too much time obsessing over my father, over why he decided to command an army instead of living with me and Mama in this beautiful city. I thought that if even he, having left us, had failed, I, too, would make an irreversible mistake sooner or later. But war changes people, their relationships—no one comes out unharmed. Zia Rosa and Mama formed an alliance and raised us on stories and songs. Fables aren't all that different from real life. It's the commander of the river's duty to protect the people of the village from the crocodiles and, to do so, he can only rely on his ability to distinguish good from evil. Will he succeed in this extremely difficult role?

After everything I've gotten into, I'll admit that, deep down, I knew all too well how everything had unfolded. It's one thing to sense the truth, another to actually say it out loud. My mother washed her hands of it and sent me there alone, as a scout. In my opinion, certain knots should be untied at home, and as I've told her many times—you need to steel yourself to face reality. But she's convinced she made the right decision, that you need to come out of your shell to make your bones.

The fact remains that I had to flunk a grade, dodge punishment, and even get hurt to find the courage. Now I'm ready. I want to narrate the events from beginning to end and explain them fully. Only by putting one word after another will I be able to make sense of everything. Sissi will be happy. I owe it to her above all—she's my little sister.

IT'S NIGHT, IT must be past two. The moon illuminates the island, which, shining like an enchanted ship filled with gold, lights up my way. It looks like it's going back up the river, which embraces the island with its sparkling, dark waters. The streetlights are out, or maybe I'm wrong—I just can't see very well.

I cross the tracks, the tram isn't running this time of night. Suddenly the sound of a siren, growing, reverberating, but they aren't coming for me, they don't even know—at least I don't think they do, since no one saw me. I walk quickly, there's not even a breath of wind. In the dampness of the river, a mouse slips into a grate. The garbage truck a little way ahead, that unmistakable rumble, it stops and loads a trash bin, turns it upside down, and the compactor kicks into action.

Sycamores along the river, hundreds of them, close in around me like foggy ghosts, more crop up with each step. I can only see out of my left eye, the fingers of my right hand are damp. I touch my face and feel something wet above my eyelid. My hand fills, the blood slides down my wrist, it flows down my forearm, but there's nothing I can do about it.

The shaved-ice kiosk by the bridge is closed. I would've asked for some ice otherwise. I wonder if their block of it has completely melted. It doesn't matter, I'm almost there. Suddenly I can't see out of the other eye either; the kiosk, the yellow traffic lights, the enchanted ship, the trees—everything is black. Down below the river spins whirlpools, it enters the city and envelops it. I cling to the parapet with both hands, the marble is cool, I can lean against it. There are iron chairs secured with a chain, but I should keep going.

The blood is everywhere, on my face, my T-shirt, a drop with each step.

I feel like Hansel and Gretel. They scattered bread crumbs so they wouldn't lose their way home. Poor fools—if your father decides to abandon you, why turn back?

I start shivering and slide to the ground. I imagine the seagulls perched on Tiber Island, in the middle of the river, and say to myself: You have to make it, you're almost there. I'm already on the bridge, a few more steps and I'll get to Fatebenefratelli. It doesn't look like a hospital, the way it's surrounded by pine trees. With its flower-filled balconies, the orange paint, those elegant cast-iron lampposts—it looks more like a grand hotel. There's the sky up there, a shining bed of stars.

Let's hope it rains tonight. I want it all cleaned up, to leave no trail. I hear the seagulls screeching, the rapids roaring, whirling, and the island—the river is mangling it.

I'm on the ship now too. The stern, turned toward the sea, is gently rocking. The moon keeps growing until it fills the sky.

A seagull hovers over me; its white wings, ever whiter and brighter, circle around me and expand.

A light, the face of a woman very close to me. Brick-red lips, black-framed glasses, hair under a net. She's a doctor, she's wearing a white coat. I'm lying on a slightly tilted gurney.

"Okay, he's coming to."

I try to sit up.

"Don't move!"

I'm attached to an IV.

The woman moves away slightly. "I'm almost done."

She has a needle and thread pulled tight, she's sewing together the flaps of the wound near my eyelid.

"What happened to you?" she asks with a sidelong glance.

I don't answer.

"They found you right outside."

"I fell."

"Where?"

"Dunno, I can't remember."

She grumbles in response, then asks the nurse to give me some meds and fill out the forms.

"Hopefully it'll come back to you, huh? Are you cold?" What a stupid question, it's probably a hundred degrees. "We'll put you in the hall for now and find you a room later."

"I can't go home?"

"Don't even think about it." And, turning back to the nurse, "Honestly! Kids these days—they're so oblivious."

The nurse who pushes my gurney into the hallway is short with stubby hands and a snake tattooed on her arm.

"Can I sit up?" I beg. She doesn't even respond. She wheels me over by the wall and blows out of the corner of her mouth to move her hair away. I try to sit up. I bend my right arm.

"Careful with the IV!" The needle goes deep. I break into a cold sweat, black in my eyes again.

"Try to sleep."

The nurse disappears behind a door. Now there's only a sliver of light. Other rooms open onto the hallway, who knows if there's anyone in them? I'm scared, I picture intubated old people covered in bruises.

I try to be brave. In a few hours, you'll feel better, I tell myself.

The blood has dried, and my T-shirt is hard against my chest. Yes, soon I'll get up and go home. I'll take a nice long shower and try to wash my clothes, or I'll throw them out—all before Mama comes back. She won't know I left, or maybe she will—maybe my aunt has already called to tell her.

"Your son couldn't even be bothered to say goodbye." I smile at the thought—how gratifying! The pain has eased a bit, I guess because of the IV.

I can almost see their faces: "But he left all his things!" The series of questions for my cousins—"Did you know he was leaving?" "What time did he go out?" "What did he tell you?" And the comments about my mother—"A traitor, just like her!"

I hear the breath of the river around the island and dream I'm in a small wooden boat, but I can't find the paddles. Only at sea can it be so pitch-black. I'm huddled up at the stern. I try to push with my pelvis, but the boat doesn't budge, the sea is still. My arms get nowhere in the emptiness, they can't reach the water.

The door opens. I must've yelled out.

"What's wrong?" the nurse asks and comes closer, feeling my wrist, then my forehead—I'm out of breath, and my heart, I feel it drop.

"I had a nightmare."

"Just relax, everything's fine."

No, everything is not fine, I'm still in the hospital. I wanted to wake up and see that it was all a dream. As has happened many times before.

Mama would turn on the lights. She'd find me sitting up in bed, hands fumbling in the dark. Her voice was enough to calm me. She'd bring me a glass of water. "The usual dream?" she would ask, but there wasn't a usual dream. I'd feel around, breathing heavily, as though trapped by the walls. I'd feel restricted, locked in a trunk. Things like that.

"Excuse me," I call out to the nurse as she walks away.

"Yes?"

"I'm sorry, I was just wondering if I maybe still had my backpack when they found me."

"I put it under there for you. What do you need?"

"My phone, to make a call."

"You want to call home?"

"Not right now, I don't want to alarm anyone."

"As you wish. Later the eye doctor will see you, and we'll find out if everything's okay."

I have no intention of calling my mom, that's the last thing I need. It's just that time seems to have stopped.

"When will the eye doctor see me?"

"When he gets here, I'll take you to him, all right? It's not even six o'clock."

"But what do you think—is it serious?"

"I don't know. The doctor will be able to determine that when he examines you. Maybe you can tell him what happened."

"Does it look bad to you?"

"Well, it's not looking good."

"Really?"

"Really. Come on, don't waste my time. I'll be back soon."

The woman walks away. Thankfully it's not so dark out anymore, the sun is starting to rise.

It feels like an eternity has passed when they come back for me. This one is a different nurse, also short, but she has a crew cut and her hair is bleached.

"Where's the other nurse?"

"She finished her shift."

"And she didn't come say goodbye?"

"You think we have time to say goodbye to all our patients?"

"She said she'd bring me to the eye doctor."

"Instead I'm bringing you. Sit up." She rolls a wheelchair toward me and gives me a signal with her eyes.

"I'm not going to sit in that. I'm no old person, I can walk."

"Hospital rules. Come on, everyone deserves to be wheeled around once in a while."

I feel self-conscious about the state I'm in—all dirty, my eye bandaged, and pushed around like a paraplegic by a woman who could be my mother. I sit hunched over with my eyes down. It's almost 8:00 a.m., and the hospital is packed. In the central courtyard covered by a transparent ceiling, a woman asks the newsvendor the price of a magazine, and nurses and visitors indulge in cappuccinos and cornettos at the café counter. The desks are arranged in a circle, and people wait their turn to pay their co-pay. We take the elevator to the fifth floor. The nurse steers me down a labyrinth of hallways to the ophthalmology department. The waiting room is accessed through a glass door, there are two long rows of chairs lined up against the walls.

"They'll call for you. I'll come back for you in a bit."

"It'll still be your shift?"

She faintly curls her upper lip: it'd take much more to provoke her.

"I'll come back for you," she simply repeats.

After about half an hour, a doctor comes out and calls my name. He's wearing a green coat, a bandanna of the same color covers his forehead. A few white hairs sprout from his neck. He's tall and thin like me. He moves lightly in his orange clogs.

"I'll stand up, Doctor, I can do it."

"Don't trouble yourself, I can handle it."

He pushes me into the room, a colleague is sitting behind the desk. Little round glasses, white coat, and tie—finally a normal-looking guy. But I can tell from his demeanor that it's actually the one with the bandanna who knows best.

"Okay, let's see what happened to this handsome young fellow," he says, pulling out the medical report. He puts on some blue-framed reading glasses.

"They brought you into the ER unconscious." He lifts his eyes to study me above the lenses. "What happened?"

"I don't remember, Doctor. I passed out."

"You don't remember?" He chuckles and takes a few steps toward me. "All right . . . so let's see this eye of yours," he says, pulling on gloves. He focuses on the stitches on my cheekbone and eyebrow for a moment; the latex sticks to his hands. Then he removes the gauze and rips off the bandage.

"A pretty nasty blow," he murmurs to his colleague, who continues writing, minding his own business.

"Have you ever had problems with your eyes before?"

"No, I've always seen fine, Doctor."

"No exam, no glasses prescription?" He examines me from above his lenses.

"When I was little, but everything was fine. Oh—one time I had a sty."

"Good, now come sit over here."

Finally, with a nod, he allows me to stand up. But only for a moment: I get out of the wheelchair to immediately sit back down in front of a strange contraption.

"What is this?"

"It's called an ophthalmoscope."

The doctor studies the injured eye, he sees it reproduced on a computer screen. My forehead is pressed up against the space machine. It emits blue rays. I hold my breath as though it might somehow influence the results. I wish he would make some comment, but he only tells me where to look. Right. Left. Down. Up. My eye feels as heavy as molten lead. I feel it explode, collapse into the socket—I can no longer see a thing.

"Doctor, what's wrong with me?" I'm getting anxious.

"Are you sure you don't want to press charges? If you decide to, you only have twenty-four hours to do so."

"Press charges?"

"Is there anything you're afraid of?"

"Afraid? Of what, Doctor?"

"This isn't an injury you get just by falling. Tell me the truth—I've been seeing a lot of fights these days."

His colleague, who until then hadn't said a word, tries to scare me: "Look, it's worse for you this way. The less you say, the more time it'll take to treat you."

I definitely prefer Doctor Bandanna. Now he's started scribbling furiously, and I'm back in the wheelchair.

"We have to run some tests."

"What does that mean?" I'm starting to panic. "Is it serious?"

"My dear boy, I can't answer that right now. Let's do the tests first."

He puts the bandage over my eye again, stands up, throws the door open—the nurse with the platinum mohawk is already there.

"Are we heading back down to the ER?" I ask. "I have to go to the bathroom."

"Okay, I'll take you."

We're in the first-floor hallway again, thankfully there are no old people full of tubes. The nurse slips into a storage room, coming back with my things. I rummage through my backpack, hoping I have at least one clean T-shirt. In my rush, I didn't pack much. I was afraid they'd catch me if I went out with too big a bag. Instead, I left quietly, pretending I was just going for a walk. I find a red polo shirt, no pants—better than nothing. My phone, in the front pocket, is dead.

"Is there an outlet around here somewhere?"

"Yes, but right now you don't have enough time to charge it. If you want to make a call, you can use the hospital phone."

"I don't have the number memorized," I lie. I feel lost without my phone.

"Go change in the meantime."

She lets me go into the bathroom without the wheelchair. Taking off my T-shirt is a challenge—I have to stretch out the collar to avoid my eye, extend the arm punctured by the IV, and lift it up over my head very slowly. The entire procedure takes several minutes. I'm out of breath, I've broken into a cold sweat. It must be the drugs. Who knows what's in that IV? I start feeling hungry, I haven't eaten since yesterday.

The nurse knocks. "Everything okay?"

"Yeah, all good. I'll be right out." I turn on the faucet and put my wrists under the cold water—my Zia Rosa taught me this, a remedy against low blood pressure. Then I dab my cheeks, forehead, and chin with a wet paper towel. Good thing there's no mirror. I taste something bitter in my mouth, a white film. I didn't even bring a toothbrush. I try to drink using my hands, but my throat is closed, I struggle to swallow.

Again, a knock at the door.

"Everything okay in there?"

I walk out and take a seat back in the wheelchair.

"What do you say, do we want to make this phone call?"

"But what time will I be done?"

"That I don't know."

"Then it'd be better if I called now."

"Oh, so you've got your memory back!"

She returns, wielding some kind of gigantic remote control.

"What is that?"

"It's a cordless. Don't worry, it still works." She chuckles.

I wait until she walks away and dial Zia Rosa's number. I don't think she'll pick up, it's her home phone, and she leaves for work really early in the morning. Better this way, she'll hear the message when she gets back.

"Zia, Auntie, it's me—I'm at Fatebenefratelli Hospital. Don't tell Mama, everything's okay. My phone's dead. I'll call you later."

Maybe I shouldn't have called. There's no way she won't tell my mother.

The nurse comes back in, then shuttles me from one room to another.

"Now what?"

"A bed has been freed up. I'll take you upstairs, they're about to serve lunch. Were you able to get through to your mother?"

I make an unintelligible movement with my head that Platinum Mohawk interprets as a yes.

I'm not hungry anymore, I throw myself on the bed as I am. I crash immediately.

I dream about an enormous airplane—the door open, no stairs leading up to it. I walk around the plane, and it transforms into a very tall building, inaccessible. I should leave. Where did the plane go? There it is again, an old white wreck, stairs made of bricks. I climb them and find myself in an empty room with no chairs, just two little windows at the back through which you can make out the sea. At some point my father and mother appear, they're sitting next to each other. Drinking tea. "Good thing," they tell me, "you survived; the plane you missed fell out of the sky." They keep talking with each other as if nothing were wrong, but our aircraft is thrown off balance, it's tilting forward, we're plummeting down toward the sea, we'll never be able to get back up to the surface, I'm going to die with my parents.

I open my eyes.

Zia Rosa is next to me, squeezing my hand.

"Zia. When did you get here?"

"About an hour ago."

"You should've woken me up!"

She smiles. She looks drenched, as if she'd just come out of water.

"What, is it raining now?"

Even her hair looks wet. "No, it's not raining."

"What happened? It looks like you're melting." The thing is Zia Rosa never sweats, or at least I've never seen her sweat. "Did you swim to the island?"

"Quit it, wise guy. It's just two drops on my forehead. You almost gave me a heart attack."

"Who told you where I was?"

"The receptionist downstairs. What happened?"

"Have you talked to Mama?"

"Not yet. I first wanted to see how you were. She'll be back in a few days; she took a week of vacation. Will you tell me how you ended up in the hospital?"

"It was nothing, just a bad fall. Where did Mama go?"

"To the Dolomites, to hike. We were supposed to go together, but my knee still hurts. Just a bad fall you say, huh?"

Zia Rosa stands up and turns to head out of the room. "Where are you going?"

"To get some air, I can't breathe in here." Out of the corner of my eye, I can see her walking away down the hallway. She's still limping. It's been over two months since she stopped running.

2

ZIA ROSA USED to run along the river every day around lunchtime. She would've preferred the morning, but Sissi started school early, and they couldn't make it in time to run eight kilometers, come back, take showers, eat breakfast, and leave again.

When we were kids, she went on her own—it's only been a few years since Sissi started tagging along. You can tell how much that girl adores her mother; she does whatever it takes to be near her.

Sometimes Zia Rosa had to stay late at work to make up the hours, or she'd take a Saturday shift. It didn't bother her, she's always liked being a librarian.

They would go home together and change: tank top and hat during a heat wave, windbreaker on days with a north wind. They'd begin their run along Via Marmorata, cross the Porta Portese Bridge, and then go down the ramp.

There's a bike path down there along the riverbank, a strip of asphalt between cobblestones and cement. When the weather's nice, everyone pours out onto the path: Sunday runners, police on horseback, cyclists, children on Rollerblades, little old people, and ladies walking their dogs. They'd run all the way to Castel Sant'Angelo, then turn back—a stretch where the river runs through the most beautiful part of the city. The path is airy, and caper bushes grow all over the massive walls. One afternoon, Sissi got the idea in her head to pick some, and seeing as they were too high up, it became my job to lift her onto my shoulders. You wouldn't believe it—she nearly broke my neck just for some tiny, tasteless buds.

When it rains, the path fills with puddles. To avoid them, Sissi and Zia Rosa would run on the grass instead, or straight through the puddles, splashing everything. I'd follow them at a distance on my bike.

My mom had been the one to insist, after they'd murdered that paparazzo under the Testaccio Bridge: "I always said the Lungotevere trail was dangerous."

"You watch too much TV," Zia Rosa had responded, laughing. Still, she appreciated my going with them.

After checking for any shady characters, I would sit and wait for them in my favorite place, just beyond the Porta Portese Bridge. The vegetation is wilder the closer you get to the sea, and it no longer feels like you're in the city. That's where you meet the real inhabitants of the river—people who have nothing in common with one another other than the fact that they're alone and very poor. The African man always leafing through old magazines, the Gypsy girl with her two children, the old woman with extremely long white hair, the Bengali couple holding hands. They all stock up on water from the Ripa Grande fountain and march back single file, carrying the buckets on their heads. Sometimes you can hear their voices behind the bushes, and if you're ever around when it's dark out, you'll see scattered lights.

In that place, the walls look like white slides, enveloped up top in tangles of fig trees, oleanders, oak trees, and other plants I don't know the names of. One of the steep side walls is bare; it's where people come to skateboard. That was exactly where I sat down in the spring—on the slabs of travertine where the snapdragons sprout—and waited for them, opening and closing the half-bloomed flowers between my fingers. I'd never thought about running myself, and Sissi would constantly make fun of me for how I'd sit, staring at the water, lost in thought.

There are more birds living on the banks of the Tiber than you might expect. You only need to sit still for a bit and you'll start hearing them sing from the branches—it's like they're chatting. Birds with little masks around their eyes appear out of nowhere, and others with shiny green and blue feathers. In the thick of the reeds or gliding on the water's surface, there are ducks and black moorhens with red beaks. The cormorants, on the other hand, quickly locate their prey and dive in from above, then rest, satisfied, to dry off.

Sissi didn't believe me when I told her about the birds. She thought it was an excuse not to listen to her.

"Why don't you just try? Everyone can run."

"I don't feel like it, Sissi. I'd last five minutes max!"

"You just have to push on until you hit your stride. At a certain point, your legs move on their own, believe me, as fast as the river!"

I didn't fall for it, not even when she told me about the incredible things that always took place in my absence, coincidentally. "You won't believe what you missed. The strangest things happen when you aren't there!"

Like that time, for example, when they saw cloth dummies being thrown from a bridge and some crazy people singing at the top of their lungs, as though acting out an ancient ritual. Or the day they'd come across a procession of roosters that, in the blink of an eye, had encircled them, scampering arrogantly.

"That's crazy! You're making this up."

"Maybe there's someone raising them nearby," suggested Sissi, a sly expression on her face.

"Yeah right, the hobos sleeping under the bridges!"

"Look, I'm not joking. They surrounded us and began pecking at us."

"It's true," Zia Rosa confirmed.

Anyway, she was so insistent that I decided to indulge her. Just this once. After locking my bike to a pole, I showed up at the bottom of the ramp with shorts, gym shoes, and a lit cigarette.

"Finally!" said Zia Rosa.

"Throw that cigarette away immediately!" Sissi yelled, snatching it from me. "Can't you read the package? Smoking kills!"

Her mother was jumping up and down in place and enjoying the scene. "He'll quit, believe me, just as soon as he gets into running. Come on, let's move."

"You know what my science teacher said?" Sissi asked me, also gesturing for us to start. "That when you're young it's even worse!"

"Wait, why? Because when you're old it's good for you?"

"No, but at that point, you've already done all the damage you can do to yourself."

We were off, and after not even five minutes, I was winded, while Zia Rosa and Sissi continued chatting comfortably.

Watching them, it didn't seem like they were running, but enjoying a nice stroll. I plodded along to keep up with their pace, and Zia Rosa encouraged me to no end: "It's normal, you just have to push through." So I put my whole self into it, panting more and more.

There were hundreds of swallows flying under the arches that day, over the open river, a scene you wouldn't believe. One time I read that for some groups of people, these birds symbolize freedom and eternal happiness and that anyone who dares to kill one will go blind.

Suddenly something on the water's surface caught my attention, a tremor of many small circles. And sure enough, there was a swallow in that very spot—it was drowning. It thrashed about, beating its wings. Then, as though feeling compassion or maybe just shock, I stopped in my tracks, as did Sissi and Zia Rosa. My heart was beating hard and fast, while the little bird moved farther and farther away, forcefully dragged by the current.

"I'm going to jump in and save it!" I yelled out.

Zia Rosa, touching my shoulder lightly with the palm of her hand, quickly countered, "No, you aren't. With all the mice in the Tiber, you'd surely get typhus, which would really be absurd in this day and age."

Since there was nothing we could do, Sissi and Zia Rosa resumed running. I'd hoped we were done, but I didn't complain because I did not want to stand there in a daze to watch the swallow die.

We went at a good pace for over a kilometer, coming across people running in the other direction from time to time: a chubby guy determined to lose weight, an American student with a Columbia University T-shirt, and an old marathon runner, lean and gnarled like a tree trunk.

The exertion made me feel like a dinghy about to burst, whereas Sissi looked sad, I'd even say miserable, so Zia Rosa began telling us a story.

The protagonist dives into the Tiber to save a swallow and carries it back to the riverbank to dry. The boy wasn't afraid of catching any diseases, and he obviously cared about the swallow, at least at the beginning of the story, "when he still had a heart."

"Why, then what happens?" asked Sissi.

"What happens is the boy gets bigger. Then one day he sees a child drowning in the river and doesn't lift a finger."

"That can't be true!"

"Well, he'd grown up, he'd lost his innocence. He'd been in prison for a few years, and it completely changed him. They'd made him think that in order to survive, you must mind your own business without wasting any time to help your neighbors. Work, put some money aside, make a fortune. What did he care about saving a young boy?"

Sissi grew even sadder.

"Do you know what this story teaches us?" continued Zia Rosa, carried away. "That we must stay true to our ideals, because opportunism corrupts the souls of simple people, making them selfish and blind."

We'd been running again for about ten minutes, and maybe precisely because she was telling the story with such passion, she tripped on a loose cobblestone. As she fell, she opened her arms wide like a large bird, losing her balance almost to the point of slipping into the river.

Sissi yelled out, "Mama!" and burst into tears.

But Zia Rosa popped right back up and, to reassure us, said it was nothing. She limped without complaining and almost started laughing: "How about that? Thanks to a swallow, I almost ended up in the Tiber."

But her knee looked like a red balloon that evening, a purple balloon the next morning, a black balloon by the afternoon—so she decided to go to the doctor.

Now Zia Rosa still limps, but I know she'll get better, everyone knows her knee will be okay. Sissi, however, has not been the same: she'd never imagined that sooner or later she'd have to run alone.

That girl might seem extremely strong, but I know her—even Sissi gets scared sometimes. When we were kids, she always wanted to kick the ball around with me and my friends. She'd follow me all the way to the field, dressed to play. At times, I'd feel angry about how good she was at getting unmarked, and so I'd tell her to go away because she was a girl and there were already too many of us. She'd go and sit on the steps, all upset. I'd feel guilty and would call her back onto the field to join my team—that's how she got better and better over the years.

After Zia Rosa's fall, Sissi lost all sense of proportion. By her own logic, she told me that since her mother wouldn't be able to train with her for a while, from that moment forward I had to take her place.

I didn't simply have to accompany her, no, I had to run with her—because running alone is hard, it's scary, running alone is impossible.

I swear I tried another couple of times, and now I know it's not true that you get into your stride and everything becomes easier. "But you're so tall and thin!" insisted Zia Rosa, as though strength and will weren't needed to handle legs that felt like boulders, all the heavy breathing, and the lack of a true objective.

After a while, Sissi got sick of begging me and tried recruiting her friends instead. I'd see them walk down from the bridge wearing all different colors, cheerfully chirping, telling who knows what secrets. But it wasn't long before she was already ahead, increasingly out of reach, and her friends were behind, gasping for air. I was there, sitting somewhere or riding my bike as her escort, but she'd scarcely so much as glance at me.

In the end, disappointed in my and her friends' lack of enthusiasm, she gave up on our company altogether.

Sissi thinks that everything is connected—humans, nature—and she's obsessed with symbols. According to her, running is about perseverance, because in all areas of life, if you aren't tenacious, you won't get anywhere. The fact is that you must make certain decisions on your own; other people can't be the ones to convince you.

As soon as I heal, maybe I'll try again.

3

"I BROUGHT YOU shaved ice."

"Black cherry, orange, and coconut?"

She nods.

Zia Rosa sets the cup down on the table. We're outside, out in the open.

"It's nice here. It doesn't even feel like a hospital."

There's an opaque glass door partway down the hallway my room is on. It leads to a fairly large balcony with pots of roses and geraniums along the perimeter. Less critical patients are allowed to receive their visitors in the fresh air, seated around the little plastic tables.

I stir the coconut pieces into the ice. The paper napkin wrapped around the cup is soaking wet.

"When did you get back?" Zia Rosa has her right hand on the table, her shoulders slumped.

"Yesterday."

"You could've at least let us know." She sighs. "You need to call your mother."

"I will, later."

"She should hear your voice, not mine. Otherwise, she'll get even more worried."

We sit in silence, I drink through the straw. The syrup is sweet, the ice is melting fast. A bit of relief, even if my head is still pounding. I'm nauseous—noises and sounds are all amplified. I feel an endless weakness, as though my body and mind are no longer responding to commands. I let myself go.

"Zia, will you tell me something about your mother?"

"Why are you asking me this?"

"Do you still remember her?"

"You already know this, I've told you so many times. She died when I was a child. All I have left are a couple photos." She adjusts the scarf around her head. She always does this when she's agitated—she unties and ties again.

"So now what memories do you have of her?"

She stands up and sets both hands on the table, leaning forward.

"You're asking because of your father, aren't you?"

"Mama threw out all his photographs. I don't even know what he looks like anymore."

I feel my face burning, the pain sharpening. Zia Rosa moves her chair closer to mine, and together we look at the building facing us.

"It's strange, when I think about my mom, I always picture her with schoolbooks under her arm even though I never saw her like that. But that's how she met my father, when she was still just a girl."

"He was her teacher, right?"

"Yes. Back in those days many schools in Mogadishu were Italian. Papa had been living in Somalia for a few years. Mama was a lot younger—"

"And then they got married!"

"Yes, but she was already sick . . . I was born less than a year later. My father was afraid I'd get infected, so he had her quarantined. But I've already told you these things."

"Did you ever get angry at your father?"

"Angry?"

"Because he wouldn't let her be with you?"

"He'd say that Mama had to get better and that as soon as she was well, she'd come home. I missed her. I still remember her voice. And my father—a man too old for a daughter my age—spent all his time with Italians, people just like him."

"And when you grew up you got angry?"

"Yes, somewhat. I had a better understanding of how things worked. In part thanks to your mother. Remember those Somali relatives she helped me track down?"

"Who? The aunt in Denmark?"

"Yes, my aunt told me many people recovered from tuberculosis. The real problem was that Mama didn't take care of herself."

"They didn't make them take their medicine in the sanatoriums?"

"They did, but apparently Mama kept running away. The last thing she wanted was to be locked up. Who knows if it's true. I like to think she was trying to get to me."

"Maybe she was."

"But to come home she had to take her medicine . . . It's hard. Sometimes people make stories sound more dramatic than they already are. Anyway, that isn't what I blame my father for."

"So what do you blame him for?"

"I was seven years old when Mama died. We immediately moved to Italy and lost touch with our relatives down in Somalia. Papa seemed relieved, and he began saying awful things about Somalis, things like they're always asking for something, that they're opportunistic. That's why he never called them, he said. Then he decided to entrust me to his sister, who was even older than he was. You can probably imagine . . . my Somali side was banned from that house."

"What does that mean?"

"Come on, you know exactly what it means."

"What?"

"That my father was a fascist!"

"But he married a Somali woman, didn't he?"

"Yes, thirty years younger than him. Let's just be done with this now, and you can tell me what the hell happened to you."

Sissi ran alone with a canister of pepper spray in her pocket. She'd bought it on eBay from an American vendor because in Italy, those sprays are illegal. She always had it on her; that weapon was almost part of her, like her nails or her teeth.

Some days, especially when school got out early, we'd head home along the Lungotevere trail, the two of us with a small group of friends. We would stop and talk just past the railway bridge.

On the other side of the river, we'd see the fire department's divers, their red motorboats, the gasometer, and two old cranes folded forward. Dressed in red and orange, the firefighters sometimes said hello, other times they got angry—using mopeds on the trail is not allowed.

Sounds echo under the bridge, and the river flows faster. We liked to stop there, right where the trail widens and the embankments look like floating beds of violet flowers with yellow hearts. In the spring, a mystery gardener even plants primroses.

We never ended up meeting him, but Sissi was so moved by it that she convinced us to fix up an old, abandoned bench. "Making this place beautiful is our job too."

Sissi is very lucky: her friends always listen to her. Of course, in the end, she's the one who takes responsibility, never anybody else. And anyone can spend a few hours painting a rickety bench. Each with their own good reason. I, for one, cared about having a place to sit.

And she's relentless. "What if I painted a mural under here?" she said one day, leaving us all a bit stunned.

Like she was decorating her own house.

"What would you paint?" one friend asked her.

Sissi showed us a drawing of someone I knew all too well: a woman with spiderwebs instead of hair.

"Who is this woman?"

"What do you mean, who is it? It's Tincaaro, the queen of the giants!" she retorted.

The portrait was so finely detailed, but painting a mural is something else entirely.

"I know how to do it. My art teacher in middle school taught us how to use a grid. Divide the drawing into many little squares, trace the blown-up grid on the wall and reproduce the drawing piece by piece. I can help you," suggested Stella Ricorsi, who was still her friend at the time.

"I'd rather try to do it by myself."

In any case, the mural was postponed a bit because we had our final oral exams, homework—and Sissi has always been one to take school very seriously.

Once vacation began, she couldn't wait to devote herself to her project. First, she had to buy the materials: primer to make the paint stick, a paintbrush, and spray paints. Then she could finally devote herself to the mural. Tincaaro was gorgeous; it looked like she could come to life at any moment. But it took a lot of time to finish, mostly because Sissi wouldn't let anyone help her.

One afternoon, we were all together under the arch, doing nothing in particular except checking in on how her work was going.

It had been raining for days. A scary amount of water was coming down, it seemed like thousands of people were pouring bucketfuls off the bridge. The river was swelling, almost reaching the edge of the trail, the grass was drenched, and the ground so slimy and claylike that it stuck to your shoes.

I smoked in silence. Our friends sat on the bench, chatting, and now and then, we'd all glance over at Sissi, who was concentrating on painting. She only had some retouches to the hair left to do at this point, and she improvised dense green coils that looked like a tangle of branches or a spiderweb.

Then, while we were all calm and relaxed, Stella Ricorsi blurted out: "Who knows what would happen if the river rose all of a sudden. Would we be able to escape?"

I imagined an enormous mass of water rising up and submerging us all. The river wanted to take possession of the city, its buildings; we disappeared under the wave and became like logs dragged by the current.

"The river could flood," a man from the Civil Protection Department had said on the news. I don't know if they always interview the same person, but when whoever it is gives the report, he's always wearing a yellow raincoat and he's always in the same apocalyptic pose: standing on a bridge with dark waters and the tops of the trees behind him.

Suddenly I felt scared, as if the river really could overflow, and I instinctively looked for the iron rings in the massive walls. I knew perfectly well that if the water level rose, it wouldn't matter that I know how to swim, the current would still carry me away.

With these thoughts, I realized Sissi had finally completed her mural, and instead of being happy, she still had the usual frown on her face. Ever since Zia Rosa had fallen and Sissi was forced to reconcile herself to running alone, she barely spoke to me, and each time we made eye contact, she turned the other way. Deep down it hardly mattered to me, but it had all gone on too long, she needed to give it a rest.

I now regret how things went. It's just that I couldn't stand Sissi being like that—she's my little sister, she can't decide out of the blue to no longer talk to me. That's why I decided to make her angry—if she wanted to fight, we had to actually fight.

A few months earlier, I'd started playing an idiotic joke. People thought I'd lost my mind, I know, but disturbing everyone was irresistible. Seeing their disbelieving faces really cracked me up.

A few months earlier, in fact, after celebrating the Day of Remembrance for the twelfth time in my schooling, I became obsessed with saying "Heil!" to everyone: the phone rang and I'd respond, "Heil! Who is it?"; cars honked when I crossed the street out of nowhere, and I'd yell "Heil!"; I'd raise my hand to leave the classroom and ask, "Heil! Can I go to the bathroom?" My teachers pretended they hadn't heard me—they knew it was one of my stunts—but one time I yelled a bit too loud and they suspended me.

Sissi finished the mural and, having gathered up her spray paints and brushes, she was about to leave without even saying ciao, so, stretching out my hand, I signaled my goodbye—"Heil! Sissi"—my arm at an obtuse angle from my body. She finally turned around—which was exactly what I'd wanted—her hair as straight as electrical cables, and she was so full of anger that her eyes seemed to nearly pop out of her head.

She came closer, furious. "You are the most disgusting being on this planet," she exploded. "You disappoint me. You never take anything seriously, you hurt the people who love you the most, and nothing but shit comes out of your mouth." And since I was watching her closely, I saw she was, almost imperceptibly, sliding her hand into her pocket with robot rigidity.

She was standing with her neck stretched forward, looking like a strange bird with a crest, and her voice was so raspy I could hardly make out the words: "I devoted myself heart and soul to helping you in school, and we're in our third year of high school, not in first grade," she screamed, tightly squeezing the pepper spray in her right hand.

And in that moment, I really don't know how to explain why, gripped by some form of rage, I kept convulsively repeating, "Heil!"

Sissi's words seemed to me amplified, while the canister came closer and closer to my eyes. She held it like a weapon: "You even got yourself suspended . . . In a few days, the charts will be posted, and you know perfectly well they'll flunk you again this year."

It was raining so hard it looked like a curtain of water, Sissi's neck was swollen with venom, and she yelled, "I hate you!"

I wouldn't stop repeating, "Heil!" while laughing hysterically like a hyena, and the gasometer in the distance looked like a whirlwind drawing nearer, lifting us into the air for the final battle.

And because I kept moving like a crazed marionette and our friends were begging me to stop—because I wasn't at all amusing—I did the worst thing I could do to calm myself, considering the weapon aimed straight at me.

The problem with Sissi is that she doesn't want to believe that we're different. She's always been convinced that, since we grew up together, everyone considers us equal. But let's be real—no one looks at me and Sissi in the same way, people's eyes see the differences, and it's not enough that we were both raised on Zia Rosa's fairy tales and my mother's songs. Being siblings by choice isn't enough either.

Sissi and I can't be equal for a whole lot of reasons, but there's one more important than the others, and it's that I'm black, born from two black parents, while Sissi is white, with golden curls and gray-green eyes. I'm black, and Zia Rosa is outwardly black, but she didn't transmit any of it to her daughter—any of her colors, I mean. Sissi's colors are those of her father and her grandfather maybe, but they aren't those of her other grandmother, Zia Rosa's mother—on her, those colors left no trace.

I thought about all of this, and in the meantime, the ground was getting muddy, Sissi's mural hadn't yet dried, the walls under the arch were damp like those of caves, and the spider woman was slowly changing shape.

Sissi didn't understand, or didn't want to understand, that brotherly love isn't enough to make a color because color is what others see, not what you see, what you feel, and no fairy tale, no song, no friendship can change the color that others see. That's why I can say "Heil!" but Sissi can't even pronounce it. "Heil!" is not taboo for me because I myself am the taboo, and it's my color, here, in this city, along this river, that's a taboo.

Sissi loved saying: "My curls are kinky like Mama's, they're like spiderwebs. That's why Mama says I'm Tincaaro. I run like Mama, and we have the build of distance runners."

And so Sissi and Zia Rosa think they run along the river like gazelles in the savanna. But this isn't the savanna—we're in Rome, this is the Tiber, there is the gasometer, Zia Rosa damaged her knee, and she may never run with her daughter again.

Sissi has golden curls and gray-green eyes and she pointed the pepper spray canister at my eyes, so I yelled out the taboo word, her taboo, and turned to disappear past the curtain of water, but she was faster than me and she pressed down to spray. She pressed down one time, maybe two, and I reached out my hands to stop her: "Sissi, it's not a toy!" The rain didn't wash away the poison, and my eyes burned. I couldn't even stand up anymore, and while I collapsed under the bridge, Sissi disappeared behind the curtain of water for good.

4

ZIA ROSA IS like a second mother to me. When Sissi and I were little, she was always the one who picked us up from school because Mama worked until seven every day, except for Saturday and Sunday.

I really liked being around them because we always came up with something new and one afternoon was never like another: special cakes on rainy days, clay sculptures of sea monsters and spaceships. We'd go wild with paints, glue, construction paper, shells, dry leaves—basically anything we could get our hands on. It's thanks to Zia Rosa I discovered I wasn't as useless at drawing as I'd thought.

I wasn't so good at depicting figures exactly as they were, or maybe I didn't make enough of an effort. I liked painting scenes as they were occurring—naval battles, cosmic wars, an army of ants—everything happened as I messed around with the paintbrush. Sissi, instead, enjoyed inventing imaginary creatures, mixing stencils of giraffes, lions, kangaroos. It's a hobby she still enjoys, and she's gotten so good at it that she can paint giant women with spiderwebs for hair or centaurs with camel bodies.

Some afternoons, before swim class, we'd stop at the café across from the pool. Seated at a table like two adults, we'd order hot chocolate in the winter and juice in the summer.

Zia Rosa was very imaginative, and once in a while she'd take us to shows or museums. Since we were little and maybe the paintings or statues didn't say much to us, she told us incredible stories that made everything seem much more exciting. Like the one about Cronus, who, afraid of being dethroned, scarfed down his newborn children.

I remember one afternoon in particular many years ago in Piazza Navona, after having visited the Cloister of Bramante. My mom had recently given us lightsabers, just like the ones the Jedis have in *Star Wars,* and we brought them everywhere with us. After chasing each other with our bright weapons, Sissi and I decided to play living statues, so we posed, frozen in combat positions. Zia Rosa tried to make us laugh, while tourists and other people walking by stopped to take pictures and even give us some change—a bit for play, a bit for real. We were having so much fun until a policeman came and, all puffed up, told Zia Rosa she was doing something shameful. She tried to explain to him, "But, sir, it's all just a misunderstanding."

And he said, "What misunderstanding? I'll give you a misunderstanding! You're exploiting minors!" A few curious people stopped to listen, and it seemed like they were staring at us with mean eyes—they hadn't understood it was a game either.

Sissi hid behind her mom. I was so furious that I would've liked to drive everyone away with my lightsaber, and I kept asking: "Why did that policeman want to give us a misunderstanding?" Zia Rosa smiled at me and said if I want to be a Jedi, I shouldn't get so mad. In fact, it's because Luke can't control his anger that his father is conquered by the dark side of the Force and turns mean.

Zia Rosa had studied to be a teacher, and that's why she has a lot of patience and is so good at telling stories. She works at the public library, overseeing the children's room. She's an activist librarian. She plans events with authors, theater workshops, readings, and it's by listening to her that I developed a passion for books.

Of all the stories Zia Rosa used to tell us, there was one we always wanted to hear over and over again. The reason why is easy for me: the main character has the same name as I do. I've never understood, though, why Sissi liked it so much too.

> *A long time ago in Somalia, there were two old and very wise men named Xiltir and Goole. One day, accompanied by their servant Shiirre, also known as Stinky, they set out west in search of a source of water. They walked for months and months under the sun and in the dust until, tired and parched, they came to the foot of a mountain. They sat down to rest, and that's when, out of nowhere, they saw the freshest water flowing between the rocks, and they drank to their heart's content. After quenching their thirst and filling their goatskins, they broke three branches off a tree and devised a pointed and forked tool called the* hagool. *With this they dug a deep and serpentine groove such that the water could be channeled until it reached their village.*
>
> *The groove soon became a river, and the wise men were welcomed home with great festivities because they had returned, bringing the gift of water from distant lands.*
>
> *Before long, the people saw that the water was plentiful, but with it came crocodiles, and the river was infested with them. The crocodiles killed the people and their animals, and therefore no one had the courage to go close to the river.*
>
> *"Along with the water, you brought us those terrible beasts," the people cried to the wise men.*

"How did this happen?" Xiltir and Goole asked themselves, looking at each other in bewilderment. "The water was so clear at the spring. How did it fill itself with crocodiles?"

Right then they saw Shiirre, the servant who had accompanied them in search of water, and remembered that he'd washed his rags in the spring and had even taken a bath in it. Stinky had immersed himself in the water, and he'd let not just three or four, not a hundred, but more than a thousand fleas fall off him. And these fleas, as they came down along the course of the river, grew increasingly big, increasingly savage, until they turned into crocodiles.

"But why did the two wise men let Stinky wash himself in the river?" I ask Zia Rosa.

"Not everything can be controlled. The two wise men were looking for water. They found a spring, dug a river, and the water came to their village. They did what they needed to do."

"Maybe it was nighttime, and they were sleeping," Sissi adds.

"But the crocodiles," I insist. "Maybe the people would've rather been without water than live alongside the crocodiles."

"Without water you can't live, Yabar. But with crocodiles you can. Crocodiles are a necessary evil, and one has to learn to live with them."

"Go on, then, when is it that they appoint the commander of the river?"

The day I got confirmation I'd been flunked for the second time, Zia Rosa called. She wanted to speak to me in person. I hadn't gone to their house in days, I hadn't seen Sissi since the afternoon with the pepper spray.

The list with the students who failed, who would be retested, and who passed was posted in plain sight in front of the secretary's office. I knew exactly what was written next to my name, but I wanted to see it with my own eyes. Luckily, none of my friends were around.

Flunking out didn't matter a whole lot to me, to tell the truth, but I had no desire to face my mother, Zia Rosa, and so on.

I'd already been at the stop for some time when the 23 came. The bus looked half-empty, and I went to sit by the central doors. I was still mulling over the word "failed" written in red next to my name when a disgusting smell of spices and other unknown concoctions reached my nose. I whipped around and saw that it was coming from an enormous pot, wrapped in colorful cloth.

People were keeping their distance—no wonder the seats around me had remained empty—while in front, near the driver, people were packed tight like sardines.

The pot was placed in the area reserved for wheelchairs, in between two women keeping it secured with their calves. The ladies were speaking loudly in their language—I don't know why they yell so loudly when they speak in their African languages—and didn't seem to care about the people glaring at them, or maybe they didn't even realize.

Unfortunately, my eyes caught theirs, and the two women smiled at me. Maybe they were thinking: I wonder if our food is similar to the food this boy's mother cooks; and the people packed like sardines were probably thinking: Surely that boy speaks the same language as they do and eats the same food, that's why he's able to stand the stench.

I was feeling more and more uncomfortable, the word "failed" imprinted on my brain, and that smell making it hard for me to breathe. There were only a couple stops left, I decided I might as well get off and go by foot. Once outside, I could still smell it on me, and it seemed like all the people I passed were avoiding me.

When Zia Rosa opened the door, her face wasn't smiling as usual. The entryway was filled with the African busts and amulets she's so proud of even though she'd bought them in nearby

Piazza Vittorio from Senegalese street vendors. There are so many that when you walk in you have to take care not to trip. And on top of all that, there's always a censer lit somewhere, burning bark, resin, essential oil—Zia Rosa claims it perfumes the house and casts out evil spirits. The problem is that, once you've crossed the threshold, you're immediately enveloped in the haze. We're always telling her she overdoes it, but she pretends not to hear.

The smell of that food was still making my head spin so much that I saw the busts and amulets dancing and I heard the drums beating, like in some voodoo rite. Zia Rosa looked like the genie of the lamp, enveloped in haze as she was, and stared at me with two unblinking eyes, as if I'd just expressed the strangest wish ever.

I really would've liked to ask her to put out the incense and take all her paraphernalia back to the store she'd bought it from, but instead I followed her without uttering a word, tail between my legs, into the kitchen.

"Well?"

I didn't know how to respond, so, just to say something, I came out with another question: "Where's Sissi?"

It took her a moment to tell me that Sissi had gone out with her friends to avoid seeing me.

Zia Rosa has a petroleum-black mane around a rather small face, and she likes to dress in seventies clothing—floral blouses and bell-bottom pants.

What did she have to tell me that was so important? She clearly wanted to give me a talking-to. I'd been flunked for the second time, they'd all told me to study, but I always do what I want, and so on and so forth. Instead Zia Rosa took the long way around. She began with the beginning of time: the swallow in the river, her no longer running, the pepper spray, and . . .

"Have you ever asked yourself why Sissi is so mad at you?"

"I don't know, Zia. I haven't done a thing to her!"

"Nothing?"

"I was just joking, but you know what she's like when she gets offended."

"Yes, I do. But you're capable of making even saints lose their patience."

"I told you, that girl with the pepper spray is a danger to the public. She nearly blinded me, you know."

"Yeah, I just confiscated it, actually. And what can you say about school?" She was about to begin a rant even beyond what my mother would subject me to.

"What can I say, Zia? They flunked me."

"And that's it? You don't care?"

"You know, if Sissi's no longer talking to me just because I flunked, I'll get mad."

"All year long, she's tried to help you with school—"

"I get it, but don't you realize I'm the one who's most upset?"

"This is the second time that you've gotten yourself flunked, honey. Do you know what failing twice means? It means throwing away two years of your life. And that's not all. Now you have to switch schools. Have you already thought about what you'll do for next year?"

Her calling me honey was a good sign; she'd softened. On second thought, though, it made me feel even worse. Zia Rosa calls you honey, and you feel like shit . . . thanks so much, I'm sorry I'm an ass and you're always so understanding and sweet. I'm sorry I'm not able to complete anything and you go to such lengths to set me back on track. Even my mother would be better than this. At least she yells, she threatens to kick me out, she shakes her belt at me, she chases me with broom in hand. She does something. At least she has some goddamn senseless reaction. She tries to make you pay for it straight away. You have no way out, so you settle your bills then and there.

On top of everything else, right then I realized that from Sissi's room, across from the kitchen, came a green light, enough to make me say to myself: Don't tell me she's been here eavesdropping the entire time! But I didn't have the courage to tell Zia Rosa her daughter was home and I knew she was hiding that fact from me.

The nausea was coming on strong again, so I asked if I could go to the bathroom even if it, too, was jam-packed with African shapes covering the walls, printed on the curtains. Seated on the bidet, I saw five round huts spinning around me, and at the foot of the stool in front of me, there were two dwarfs with enormous noses. Even my face in the mirror looked like that of an African dwarf inside a frame of shells. I felt paralyzed while everything spun and slammed into me—the African faces, the huts, the shells, and the horrendous dwarfs—everything spun and blurred, and I felt something like a vacuum cleaner in my throat sucking up what was inside me . . . my stomach, my lungs, even my heart.

At some point, Zia Rosa rapped on the door and said: "Come out, I'm making you tea!"

She'd put the water to boil on the stove with a lot of lemon peel and, basically crawling out of the bathroom, I felt like a horrendous dwarf in front of the genie of the lamp. I went to lie down on that enormous zebra-striped piece of furniture that is their couch. I looked at the white stripes, the black ones, and then everything was striped—the walls, the floor, even the air had turned zebra-striped.

5

"HADDUU CAAWA IGU yiri badda cagaha geliyoo, timaha caarada u soohoo, soo xiro cunaabiga—"

"Hooyo, you really can't stop singing, can you?"

"Listen, Yabar, would you tell me what your problem is?"

"It's not a criticism, I'm only curious . . . so, where did your passion for singing come from?"

"Are you messing with me by any chance? You're acting weird."

"No, Mama, wallaahi, when you look at me like that you make me uncomfortable, but I swear this time I'm serious."

"From when I was a little girl, I'd say. I was part of the Ubaxa Kacaanka."

"What's that?"

"The Flowers of the Revolution. We'd sing the praises of the president, of socialism, of progress at official ceremonies. We didn't understand a whole lot. We were only kids. We'd march in the parades dressed in white and blue, the colors of the Somali flag."

"And you were proud of it?"

"What do you mean? Everyone liked being part of the Ubaxa Kacaanka. It was a great honor."

"But wasn't your father against the regime?"

"Yes, but he was also a practical man, a businessman. He tried not to get mixed up in certain matters. At least not in those years."

"Did your siblings sing in the choir too?"

"No, none of them did—not the two older boys nor my sister. I was the only one in the family who had this gift."

"Your voice?"

"When we were kids, we loved going to the theater together. The most famous songs from the shows were then broadcast on Radio Mogadishu. You could even buy cassettes."

"The original tapes? I mean, you know, with the packaging and everything?"

"Sometimes you ask such nonsense questions. No, there wasn't a real recording business in Somalia, if that's what you're asking. You'd go to certain stores on Via Roma—"

"Via Roma?"

"Yes, that's what it was called. You'd tell them what you wanted, and they'd make you a copy right then and there. Stop making me lose my train of thought."

"Sorry, keep going. I like it when you tell me stories."

"If only you didn't constantly interrupt me! So I was saying . . . I'd learn the songs by ear. My siblings loved my voice."

"And did you ever think about going professional?"

"Absolutely not. It's one thing to sing in a choir or at home, but performing on a stage, in front of people, is a whole other story. Plus, unlike you, I had a knack for school."

"Ahh, I see, any excuse is good for bringing up school. What does it have to do with singing?"

"Well, Yabar, I'm a woman, and you know, not all Somali fathers back then were so open-minded they'd send their daughter to university."

"So you had to give up your calling to show yours how smart you were."

"Don't be ridiculous. If I'd been a singer, you would've already died of hunger."

"But Grandpa was happy when you graduated?"

"Two times in my life I made my father happy: the day I finished my studies and the day you were born, his first grandson. If only he could see you . . ."

"What?"

"I don't know, now that you're all grown up. I think you'd remind him of someone very dear to him. Maybe he'd be able to forgive me."

"Are you talking about what happened when you stopped singing?"

"You're making me think back on a horrible time. I wish I'd died instead . . . oh, what a blasphemous thought! Allah's will should not be questioned."

"But, Hooyo, what did you have to do with it?"

"Never mind. And to think that before that time I felt like I was so settled in Rome, like I had lots of friends. Then, from one minute to the next, I was no longer able to work. I wanted to disappear from the face of the earth. I wandered from house to house as a guest. I never even knew where the sugar was kept."

"But eventually you got back on your feet, and we met Zia Rosa and Sissi right away."

"I'd told myself I'd never sing again. But the two of them were so persistent and enthusiastic that I thought: Here's a worthy enough reason to break a vow. Have you noticed how even Sissi understands Somali at this point?"

Our house is small: one bedroom, a living room, kitchen, and bathroom. There aren't many things inside it, no African statues, no amulets. We've lived here for eleven years.

When you enter, you're already in the kitchen, which is tiny and dark—there's only the stove, the fridge, a cupboard. My mom goes shopping every three days.

The kitchen is attached to the living room, which is where I sleep. There's a big window, a ladder that functions as a coat rack, a round table, a sofa bed, and a sort of wardrobe. It's more a bookshelf than a wardrobe, my mom puts my clean clothes as well as books in it. It doesn't have doors, only a heavy curtain with gold designs.

At night, my mom always gets angry because I don't open the couch. "It'll get ruined that way," she says. "You have to put the sheets on." But I hate opening and closing it every day. I like looking out the window at night, and I feel comfortable sitting up against the back of the couch until my eyes start closing on me. The view is beautiful, the tracks of Ostiense Station disappearing off into the distance, and the light is orange and bluish.

The other room is my mother's. It always smells like jasmine. A six-door wardrobe takes up an entire wall. Mama's bed isn't very big—it's a double, I think—but it's tall and covered with pillows. There's a Formica nightstand next to it, with a butterfly-shaped lamp.

I've always slept in a transitional bedroom, it changes between night and day. In the morning, my mom sets the round table for breakfast while I'm still in bed—I see steam rising from the teapot, and it slips between the lilac-colored petals of the lilies. The lilies are fake, and they're in a vase at the center of the table.

When she first read the advertisement, TWO-ROOM APARTMENT WITH AMERICAN-STYLE KITCHEN FOR RENT, Mama knew she wanted to live in such a place. She really liked that wording: "American-style kitchen." "This way, I can keep an eye on you while I cook," she was fond of repeating.

The house wasn't exactly in good condition, but it measured up to her expectations. The rent low, and the landlord a gentlemanly old man who lives downstairs: "Signora, if you pay on time every month, you can be sure that no one will ever send you away from this place."

She couldn't ask for more. I'd just turned seven. She was already working in Dr. Ossorio's dental practice and went to great lengths to pick me up at school every day. She always brought me to work with her in the afternoon. She didn't have anyone to leave me with. I'd sit and wait for her in the waiting room, supplied with comics and snacks. Sometimes she'd let me watch cartoons on the TV. Between one patient and the next, she'd come out in her white uniform and lower her mask to smile at me.

Mama slept very little back then. After work we'd go home, she'd take off her good clothes, we'd eat, and she'd get right back up again. She wanted the house to shine. Thankfully, it was so small that it didn't take long to repaint the walls, the window frames, the doors, to repair the wardrobes, put in the lighting fixtures, and furnish it with the few pieces of furniture she'd come by. I offered to help, but she preferred that I go to bed early, so I'd fall asleep in the silence. At the time, in fact, Mama had stopped singing, and I'll even say I didn't really mind, because I can't stand music, but that's a story for another time.

It was around then that Mama and Zia Rosa met; we'd moved into the Ostiense neighborhood, near the market, just a few months before.

I'll always remember the day my teacher decided to bring us to visit the public library. Because we were still little, she asked if there were a couple parents available to accompany the group. She had us write a message in our notebooks to bring back signed. "I'll volunteer," Mama said right away. "I'll ask if they can give me the morning off from work." I was new at the school, and Mama really wanted me to fit in quickly. She hadn't had the time to meet anyone yet, and this was a good occasion for her to get involved in the life of the class. I showed my teacher my notebook: my mother was available. I was excited, I couldn't wait for that day to come.

The morning of the visit, we walked out of school lined up two by two, the teacher at the head and Mama at the tail, to make sure the group stayed together. There was also the father of one of my classmates, the one who always came by moped. We moved like a giant snake. When we got there, the librarians welcomed us.

"Good morning, children!" they said with huge smiles and led us to the children's room.

Zia Rosa, who at the time was just Rosa, invited us to sit in the folding chairs arranged in a circle. Her big black hair seemed so funny to me, and she was sitting with a foam puppet in her lap. She made his mouth move with her right hand and his arms with her left—with the help of a small stick. The doll had big eyes and hair made of colored straw, he pretended to read a book and told us a story. Mama laughed at every joke, she was happy. When it ended, Zia Rosa began a new story and asked us to go around and continue it one by one, using our imaginations. Everyone had to participate, big and small.

"I'm not very good at telling stories," Mama said when it was her turn.

"But she's a great singer!" I interrupted out of nowhere.

"Wonderful, songs are the heart of stories," Zia Rosa said.

Mama looked at me out of the corner of her eye, trembling slightly and, because she wasn't making a sound, I placed my hand on hers, as though to give her courage. After about a minute, I looked up and saw that she was taking a big breath—suddenly Mama's voice filled up the entire room.

When story time was over, they said we could have a snack and look at whatever books we wanted. Mama went over to Zia Rosa, and I ran right behind in case it wasn't already clear that I was her son.

"Hello, thank you, truly a beautiful get-together," Mama said. "My name is Zahra," she added, stroking the top of my head.

"Nice to meet you; I'm Rosa. Thank you for your voice." And they shook hands. "You're Somali, right?"

"Yes, how could you tell?"

"Well, because I'm Somali too."

There was a moment of hesitation, then she clarified: "I mean, actually I'm half—my mother was Somali, my father Italian."

"Ah, I see."

"I've seen you before, outside school. My daughter goes there too, she's in first grade this year."

The next day, when we left school, I saw Zia Rosa waving at us. She was holding a girl's hand. We rushed over to them.

"Come to Piazza San Cosimato?"

"We can't, I'm sorry," Mama replied. "I'm afraid I have to get back to work."

"What about your son?"

"I take him with me, I haven't found a better solution yet."

"He can come with us if you like."

Her daughter had two curly blond pigtails, and she looked at me, curious. "Ciao, my name is Sissi!"

My mother seemed unsure. "The problem is I don't finish until seven o'clock."

"Mama, please, can I go with them?" For as much as I tried not to show it, I got bored at the dentist's.

"You can come pick him up at our house. I'll write down the address."

She finally decided on a yes, but she still looked a bit tense walking away.

"Children, hold each other's hands," said Zia Rosa.

Mama came to get me a few hours later. She brought a box of seytuun juice and a container of bajiye. She never showed up anywhere with empty hands. Zia Rosa was appreciative, and they sat down in the kitchen to chat. Sissi and I played in the hallway with her little rubber toy animals: tigers, elephants, bears, lions, gazelles, horses, kangaroos—an entire zoo. Mama admired the house: "It's so big!" she repeated over and over without even a hint of jealousy in her voice.

"I was lucky," said Zia Rosa. "It was my father's. I would never be able to afford an apartment like this on my own."

When I got home, after having endured Zia Rosa's talking-to about failing, I found my mother pacing back and forth in the living room, speaking on the phone in Somali. I was afraid of her reaction, but I couldn't stay away forever. I ran to lock myself in the bathroom, and when I finally decided to come out, my mother had an icy gaze, but different from usual. Strangely enough, she wasn't yelling, she wasn't threatening, she was just sitting motionless on the couch, staring straight ahead. I wasn't used to seeing her like that, and it made me even more afraid, so I began nervously fiddling with the fake lilies, waiting for her to start lecturing me. What was going through her head?

At some point, she stood up and didn't say, as I was expecting, that she'd had enough of me and that she wanted to teach me a lesson. Instead, with extreme calm, she informed me that I would be spending a month in London with her sister and my cousins. Said like that, it seemed more like a prize than a punishment, but from the tone of her voice, I could tell it would be far from fun.

My mother's younger sister is the only person in the family, besides her, who lives in Europe. Mama used to be very close to her. "But she was a fool," Mama always says. "Instead of continuing her studies, she ran away from home at seventeen to elope with an idiot. I'd warned her." After the wedding, she'd left for England with her husband. He'd gone on to be a taxi driver, she a mother.

My parents and I, instead, moved to Rome in December 1990, right before the civil war broke out in Somalia. My maternal grandparents live in Kenya, while all my other aunts and uncles are scattered around America. My mom hasn't seen them since; for fifteen years, they've only spoken by phone. It's not just because of the distance, as Mama always says: "If I went to visit all the members of my family, I'd have to circle the globe!"

My aunt, however, we've gone to visit her a couple of times, but back when my father was still living with us. Just me and Mama—he wouldn't come. I was upset when I found out he'd be staying in Rome. We even tried to convince him. "Maybe we can go see the Tower of London, Big Ben, have a holiday all together," Mama had proposed.

"It's all the same outside of Somalia," was Papa's response. He seemed sad. "The only reason to travel is to see your loved ones again. It's better if just the two of you go to your sister's."

At my aunt's house, there was a constant procession of friends and relatives with lots of children. Sometimes we even went to the neighbors' houses, and it was the same everywhere we went: women chatting and children in front of the television. No one protested if we spent the entire time watching cartoons. Not even Mama resisted—she walked around the house in slippers and spent entire days listening to gossip between the kitchen and living room. After a while, though, she'd begin to lose her patience. It was because of certain topics of conversation, I imagine, but I've only recently come to understand this.

"Yabar," she'd say to me, "let's go for a walk, I need some fresh air."

The other women considered her a bit strange, and they had no problems telling her so. They always had an excuse not to leave the house: too much wind, too much rain, too many children. Every so often, Mama dragged one of my little cousins along with us, and she'd watch us from a distance while we threw ourselves down slides or on the swings. I think she was a bit sad, all alone on that bench. Maybe she missed my father or was worried about him. One day, she brought us to the pool.

"Are you going to wear a bathing suit?" they asked her, incredulous. The fact is that Mama has always been a free spirit, she went to university, she's a curious woman. She told me a bunch of times that when she was a girl, in Somalia, things were different, and that the war had turned everyone into prudes.

"My friends and I used to play tennis, we'd go to the movies, we used to swim in the sea. Can you believe it?"

Anyway, something must have happened because Mama no longer wanted to go back to London. She surely had her own good reasons for it, but at that moment I didn't understand why, after so many years, she'd decided that I had to go and, what's more, by myself.

To be honest, there was an explanation: Mama had already told me more than once that when children misbehave, Somalis have the bizarre habit of sending them to some remote relative. But I never would've thought that she would adopt the same system with me: "Your aunt says you have to spend a bit of time with Somalis to get your head back on straight. Only when you understand where you come from can you learn how to be in the world."

Looking back, I'm increasingly convinced that Mama also needed space to breathe, to spend a bit of time on her own. It can't be easy to raise a son by yourself, without a point of reference other than a sister by choice.

Up until the day before, Zia Rosa was the only person I called my aunt. I never mentioned my mother's sister, and my English cousins were nothing but a vague memory. There was a period in which, when they'd call, Mama would pass them to me, and if Sissi was nearby, she'd try out the English words she'd learned in school: "Hello!" "How are you?" "What's your name?" And she clearly felt very important. She would've liked to have some cousins abroad to talk to too. I'd describe them to her in detail and tell her that soon I would introduce them and they'd become her cousins as well, given that the two of us were siblings.

With time, those phone calls became more and more awkward because we no longer knew each other and there wasn't anything to say.

It doesn't take me long to finish the shaved ice, I was very thirsty. Zia Rosa is right there looking at me.

"Know what I'm thinking about?" I ask her.

"What?"

"About the fable with the river and the crocodiles. Mama always says that evil is all around us and sooner or later we'll have to deal with it."

"Zahra knows war, she knows what she's talking about."

"But don't you think she's too tough sometimes?"

"How so?"

"Remember when in sixth grade I was playing soccer with that team in Testaccio? True, I wasn't very good, but you and Mama always say you've got to be tenacious, so I went all out because I loved soccer."

"Right, so?"

"When we began the tournament all those fathers came to the games, and you wouldn't believe how mean they were. Every time I messed up a pass or a shot, they'd yell: 'Heyoo, bench him!' Does that seem normal to you? We were only kids."

Zia Rosa shakes her head.

"And Mama would sit there passively, not saying a word. After a few games, the coach finds out that an opposing team was using players at least two years older than us."

"That's not allowed!" Zia Rosa comments, though, in reality, she already knows the story.

"It's not possible; at age eleven you can't play anything like a thirteen-year-old. So what does the coach do? Instead of enforcing regulations, he decides we should cheat too. 'What harm is there?' he says. 'If everyone else is doing it . . . what, we're the fools?'"

"Can't argue with that kind of logic," she adds ironically.

"Just unfortunate that he put someone older in my place, and I, since that day, have never played another game."

"All right, it's unsportsmanlike behavior. But what are you trying to get at?"

"Nothing really, just that Mama sat there passively. She didn't intervene. She thought I had to handle it all on my own. 'The world is full of ugly beasts, stay strong,' she'd say. That may be true, but don't you agree that she's too strict sometimes?"

"How so?"

"Sending me off to London, for example."

"She thought it would be good for you to see your aunt and cousins again after so long."

"And that they'd throw all the truth about my father in my face? Couldn't she have talked to me about it?"

"Yabar, it's useless for you to bury your head in the sand. Deep down you've always known the truth."

6

THE PROBLEM IS I've never liked going to school. I hate studying what the teachers tell me to, spending entire afternoons doing useless homework: translating super tedious Latin passages, solving math problems, writing essays about ridiculous people that no one will read anyway. Sissi says I'm lazy and that if I used my head and agreed to follow the rules, everything would go just fine. But what are the rules? Besides, I do use my head, but to do the things I like and find interesting, such as reading books and magazines and watching documentaries on the History Channel.

All this drama began after my eighth-grade exams—Mama consulted Zia Rosa and decided to enroll me in the linguistics high school, where Sissi would be going a year later. Who knows why our mothers were convinced they shouldn't separate us, not even for high school? And why the linguistics high school? "I think it's a good fit. I can't see you at a vocational school with all the punk kids, you're too sensitive!" Sissi commented while paging through the course packet, intrigued.

The whole story about how I was too sensitive for vocational school was made into a state matter: it was all my mom talked about, as soon as I set foot in Zia Rosa's house, it was the single topic of conversation, and even my friends, who had never before spoken to me about school, expressed their point of view. There was a full-blown firing squad aiming at me, dedicated to the cause of getting me to enroll in the linguistics school. So I started going to that awful place, and it was one of the stupidest things I've ever done. The truth is that Mama and Zia Rosa weren't ready to give up exchanging opinions on our teachers, sitting together at annual meetings, commenting on the school curriculum—in short, they absolutely did not want to stop breathing down our necks.

But above all it has to do with their connection, how else can I explain it? Mama helped Zia Rosa rediscover a part of herself, buried away for so long. She taught her how to cook Somali rice, the names of the ingredients, the meanings of song lyrics—all things Zia Rosa thought she didn't know and yet they resurfaced, bit by bit. They were just hidden away in some deep, dark corner inside her. At the same time, Mama and I had no roots in Rome, no family nearby, no long-standing friendships—connections that Sissi and Zia Rosa had no shortage of. Therefore, by connecting, they each made up for their own deficiencies.

One night when we were still little, Zia Rosa was really craving sambusas—triangular puff pastry wraps filled with meat and vegetables. So many years had passed . . . when had she last eaten them?

"Wonderful," Mama said. "We have the ingredients, I'll teach you how to make them right now!" Zia Rosa seemed like a little girl again, she was so happy. They let us stay up while they busied themselves in the kitchen, even though it was already late. Sissi and I watched a cartoon, stretched out on my sofa bed. Mama lent Zia Rosa one of her old diracs, a threadbare tunic she wore in the house. They listened to music, kneaded, and laughed like lunatics. The hot, crispy sambusas were our midnight snack. I think it's still our favorite food, mine and Sissi's, at least.

Anyway, to get back to school, let's just say I managed to pass the first two years of high school. "By some miracle," Sissi always says. Maybe she's right, but why does she have to keep repeating it?

The third year instead, not surprisingly, they flunked me: the subjects had gotten harder, and even my favorite teacher, the one for Italian, had had enough of interrogating me only on topics of my choice. It was time for me to start studying properly. The problem wasn't that I had to repeat the year, but that I'd ended up in class with Sissi, who, besides being good at all the subjects, acts like a little know-it-all and always thinks it's her job to save people.

It was unbelievable: the whole year, she did nothing but nag me—at school and at home, and that's not all . . . she was a snitch too, reporting everything I did to our moms. This meant that for the last few months of the school year, given that the risk of getting flunked a second time was growing more and more concrete, they forced me to study with her every afternoon.

Sissi is too disciplined. Every day, she follows the same strict and extremely boring routine: she comes home from school, eats lunch with her mother, studies from four to six, goes running on alternating afternoons, and twice a week she has piano lessons, which also take up a lot of time.

When she starts studying, she gets some sesame sweets from the pantry and keeps them next to her. In our houses, there's always a pack of them somewhere. Up until recently, sisins were hard to find in Italy—now they're being sold everywhere. They remind my mom of when she was young. She likes to tell us about the girl her age who, in front of their elementary school, had a glass jar full of sisin balls and sold them for few kumi each. That's what our mothers are like, they always have a story to tell. I love their stories, but sometimes they become counterproductive: Sissi will ruin her teeth with all those sisins.

The problem with school is that it makes you hate even the things you used to find interesting. Then when there's Sissi in the mix, staring at me and remarking: "You're such a slacker. I started my homework two hours ago, not like you and your always-waiting-till-the-last-minute," even that small desire to study I once had disappears completely.

One time I was sick of pretending to review, so I stood up and announced: "I'm done! I'm going for a walk."

Sissi doesn't do half measures, that girl takes things way too seriously. She forcefully pulled me back by the arm, yelling: "You're not going anywhere!"

"What're you gonna do about it? I'm a free spirit," I countered, freeing myself from her grasp. "I have it written in my DNA. I'm programmed to ride horseback through the savanna, to herd camels and drink their milk. My life was supposed to be that of the nomads: I would've gone on strolls with my camels without disturbing anyone and drunk tea under the acacia tree with my comrades. It's not my fault that wars and financial reasons took me far from my natural habitat."

Sissi pinched me in response, but she couldn't manage to stay serious either. Unfortunately, she'd gotten it into her head that with her help I'd pass; not even Zia Rosa was able to discourage her: "It all depends on him, you know, you can't keep at him so much."

"Don't you start now too!" Sissi would respond and go right back to monitoring me like a drillmaster. My little sister truly has a calling for impossible missions, and I love her for it, but how is this my fault? I tried and didn't succeed—I'm so sorry I let her down.

The balance was completely upset when Stella Ricorsi began studying with us as well. Sissi is too attached to her mother to have a best friend, but she got along well with Stella Ricorsi at the time. They were desk mates, and they shared tips and secrets. Plus, when it comes to studying, those two think alike.

Stella Ricorsi is the type of girl who on winter nights goes around with the Salvation Army handing out blankets and warm meals to hobos, she's one of those noble beings devoted to good and justice. She made me feel calm, her certainties reassured me. Surely no one had ever told her the story about the crocodiles.

One afternoon, I was reading a novel that had been assigned as homework. It was an old book with a hard, blue cover that my favorite teacher had checked out from the library. The main character of the story is named Alessio, and he always has a red carnation in his buttonhole. He's fond of it because his sweetheart gave it to him. One day, he has a conversation with his best friend who insists on the fact that becoming a man means following the same routine day in and day out. A simple reflection, but it filled me with a deep sadness. If that's the way things were, I, certainly, would never become a man. Then, though, I thought that maybe with Stella Ricorsi I wouldn't mind doing the same things every day: waking up in the morning, drinking coffee together, going to work, returning home to tell each other about our days with a nice glass of wine.

Stella Ricorsi began joining me out on the balcony to smoke and, since Sissi complained that we always made excuses to take a break, we decided to meet up on our own time on Tiber Island.

We sat in the sun, where the rapids interrupt the river's slow flow. There's a spot where the difference in water level is a bit more apparent and you can see plastic bottles and branches bouncing on the surface before being reabsorbed by the current. The biggest branches caught our attention because, watching the rapids upstream, they looked like the arms of a man being dragged by the current. Where instead you saw a ruffle on the surface of the water, it meant there was a submerged branch or that it surfaced just slightly and bisected the current.

In front of us was the old Broken Bridge. That's what they call it because it no longer connects the banks but seems to appear magically in the middle of the river, a solitary arch supported by two small islands of land. They say it's the oldest bridge in Rome and that over the centuries various popes and noblewomen have committed themselves to rebuilding it, then always ended up defeated by floods and adverse fate. It has stayed there to house the seagulls, who apparently love it and make their nests in it.

I would've liked to sit on the Broken Bridge with Stella. Maybe we could've built a hideaway with eggshell lime, spent the night stretched out under the stars, and watched the things happening around us from there without being bothered.

That afternoon, Stella Ricorsi was wearing a polka-dot skirt, a pair of red ballet flats, and because she was cold, I took my sweatshirt off to wrap around her and pull her close to me. She had orange nail polish, and each nail was decorated with a tiny white daisy. Stella Ricorsi has a mouth like a flower petal, big brown eyes, and thick black hair that makes her skin look even whiter than it is. We held each other tight while staring at our toes, and we were both embarrassed. I wanted to kiss her, but I didn't have the courage.

After about half an hour of clinging to each other like that, maybe disappointed I wasn't making a move, Stella Ricorsi broke the magic by starting to talk about school. She said that if things went badly for me this year too, she'd be very sad because being flunked out of the same year twice means changing schools, and she said I should ask myself why my grades were so disastrous, that maybe it was time to reflect and find something I liked to do.

I was still stunned by her scent and by the tension caused by the desire and fear to kiss her when, I don't even know how, she began telling me about an acting class she'd been going to for a while. She was sure I'd love it. "I have it this afternoon. Why don't you join me?" I couldn't care less about the acting class, but seeing as I wanted to stay with her, I decided to go along. I didn't know if she'd already had it in her mind to bring me there, but it made me uneasy in any case, so once we'd crossed Garibaldi Bridge, I stopped at the watermelon kiosk to get myself a beer.

I hadn't even taken the first sip when Stella Ricorsi said: "Isn't it a bit early to start drinking?"

Then, to distract her, I said: "Do you know that right over there, on Tiber Island, they used to hold a watermelon carnival in ancient times? The best moment was when the watermelons were thrown into the river and the kids competed to catch them."

And, all cheerful, Stella Ricorsi commented: "How do you know so many things?"

Cantiere, the community center where the class was held, is near the tram 8 stop. A big purple bougainvillea climbs the front of the building, almost completely covering it.

Stella was a bit embarrassed about going inside while I was still drinking, so she told me: "Maybe it's better if you finish the beer outside." This made me even more nervous, but I'd already agreed to go with, so I had to listen to her.

The acting teacher had some really bright red lipstick on, and when she smiled, all the wrinkles around her lips were so pronounced they made them look like an accordion.

As soon as she saw us, she came up to Stella Ricorsi and, after whispering something in her ear that I couldn't hear, turned to me full of enthusiasm and exclaimed: "Finally we meet!" This phrase, which on its own could even seem sweet, was the clear proof that Stella Ricorsi already had it in mind to snare me.

Out of nervousness I replied: "To tell the truth, theater has never interested me!"

To which Stella said, "I told you, he's always like this."

Meanwhile the picture was becoming clearer: among the students there were some with almond-shaped eyes, some with curly hair, some with dark skin, and there was even a Gypsy—in other words, they were all "different," everyone but Stella Ricorsi.

I felt a bit dizzy from the beer and realized that those kids weren't like me, they were different but seemed happy about it.

The teacher urged me: "This isn't just an acting class. I'd say it's an exploration of identity, of memory; it's important to draw lessons from personal baggage and learn how to share them with others."

Stella Ricorsi looked at the ground. Maybe she was ashamed of me, maybe of herself, maybe of the teacher: "This is a workshop, you should think of it as your second home. I believe in all of you, in your potential, that's why I fought hard to find a free space. You don't have to pay anything to be here."

I didn't want to do a free acting class, and the beer was going straight to my head. Stella Ricorsi was trying to smile at me, and her eyes looked like the little daisies she had on her nails—they made me think of the boy with the carnation in his buttonhole and of drinking coffee together every morning. Maybe I had to be patient if I wanted to become a man.

Then Stella Ricorsi grabbed me by the hand, and we sat down with the others in a circle. The group had already met many times; they always began by reading an excerpt from the *Odyssey,* and the theme of that day was the return.

After listening to the story of Ulysses's return to Ithaca, which almost everyone already knew, the teacher asked us to say what the word "return" meant to us and if it brought to mind any event, any story that we wanted to share with the others.

A boy stood up first, my age more or less, and began telling us about how his parents were building a restaurant in the place they were from, Sal in the Cape Verde archipelago, and how they'd reestablish themselves there as soon as it was completed. They thought the island would've stayed the same as when they'd left it, but things were changing continuously and every time they went back they were shocked and disappointed. The boy had just finished talking when the teacher, giving me a telling look, asked if there was a part of Ulysses's return that I'd liked and if I wanted to recount or represent it in my own way.

I felt full of anger because I figured that no one would've cared about my response if I weren't black. I did, though, have a favorite part: Ulysses going back home dressed as a beggar and the suitors treating him badly because they still don't know who he is, not until he takes his disguise off and kills them all.

So I stood up and, while staging the scene of Antinous insulting Ulysses, still dressed as a beggar and flinging a stool at him, I grabbed a chair and threw it up in the air to show the suitors that I wasn't any old beggar but Ulysses himself, returned to Ithaca.

All the kids got scared because I'd hit one of them by accident and almost split his lip. The teacher ran to tend to him, and Stella Ricorsi rushed over to me, choked up: "Why'd you do that?" Her mascara was staining her cheeks because of the tears, and everyone was making me feel both sorry and angry at the same time: the different kids, Stella Ricorsi, the acting teacher. That's why I ran away, because I don't like feeling sympathy, and it's not my fault they got scared; it's not like I'd asked them to invite me to their acting class.

Stella Ricorsi followed me down Viale Trastevere, crying, and I wasn't even capable of telling her that I'd dreamed of doing the same things with her every day. Who knows, maybe if she'd known . . . but by then I no longer wanted it, at that moment all I wanted was to be Ulysses killing the suitors.

Sissi never heard about the acting class because Stella Ricorsi never came back to do homework with us, and anyway, there wasn't much time left until the end of the year—before long the swallow would drown in the river, and Zia Rosa would break her knee.

In the red carnation novel, I'd underlined the word "overflow." It said something like "friendship means overflowing onto someone," so I asked myself whether Sissi and I overflowed onto each other, like the river when it overflows and covers the trail with water and mud.

7

MY MOTHER ALWAYS says that Mogadishu isn't crossed by a green river like the Tiber, instead it's bordered by the ocean, all along its length. One day, when I was about three years old, my parents took me on a trip to Gezira Beach, where you could rent bungalows to shelter from the sun. Mama had filled the cooler bag with tuna sandwiches, mangoes, bananas, and ice-cold drinks.

I loved playing with the sand and splashing around in the water, but I still hadn't learned how to swim. My father, instead, was really good at it because he'd grown up near a creek.

He was wearing a pair of blue shorts that clung to his legs, and he stretched out his hands in the water, urging me to join him. The salt made me cough; I floundered. His chest and shoulders were hard and slippery, and when I tried to hold on, I'd lose my grip, while he kept moving backward. "Come to me," he simply said. "Swimming is learned through persistence." I gasped for air, flapping my arms agitatedly like baby birds when they learn how to fly.

My father, unfortunately, didn't have enough time to teach me what he knew how to do so well. After we moved to Rome, because it mattered to her, Mama signed me up for swim class five years in a row until I got good at all the strokes.

I can still remember the first time I saw the sea in Italy. We went without Papa—just me, Mama, and some friends. A walk along Ostia Lido after having visited Isola Sacra where the Tiber empties out, cloudy and dense. Her friends made fun of her because she was used to the ocean and thought that the tide could rise at any moment. "Don't put your towel near the water, or the sea will take it away."

"The sea," they told her, "doesn't come very far forward here."

It was spring: the beach deserted, no umbrellas. The sea was dirty, the sand too, but the smell of saltiness was enough to make her happy. She jumped up and down, did cartwheels. I ran after her and tried to catch her until, surprising everyone, Mama said that even though the water was cold, she was going in just the same. I saw her throw herself into the slimy sea, delirious with joy. When you're a kid, everything seems immense.

"It's dengelous!" I screamed from the water's edge. I was scared, and I called out to her, flailing my arms.

Every time she recalls this story, Mama starts to laugh. "Can you believe it, you hardly knew how to talk!"

But she doesn't tell the story about that last trip to Gezira with Papa. The new car, the music on the radio, her happily singing, and, out of nowhere, a garrison of pickups and frowning soldiers. Lined up on the right side of the road, the bodies of three men encrusted with sand. My eyes hardly reached the height of the window, yet they saw everything. My father stretched his arm back from the front seat to push my head down, then, turning to Mama, said: "Stay calm," and got out of the car. Mama immediately moved into the back seat and pressed my face into her lap. Some very long minutes followed. My father got back in the car, said goodbye to the soldiers with a hand gesture, and began driving again, turning up the volume of the radio. The music, extremely loud at that point, drowned out my parents' voices.

Just days later we would leave Somalia. It was the summer of 1990. That's how we came to Rome, like many other Somalis in the months that followed.

When I ask my mother what happened to my father, she says that there's been war in our country for fifteen years and as far as she knows he could be dead. She says it with a coldness that upsets me, so I immediately stop asking questions.

I think about my father often, about our first years together in Rome. It wasn't uncommon for him to come get me at preschool. He'd carry me on his shoulders, and I liked seeing everything from above. His shirt would get a bit dirty from my little shoes, but it didn't seem to bother him.

By that time Mama had already found a job and was trying to make new friends. Papa frequented a club. I don't remember the neighborhood, but I'm guessing it was close to Termini. It was a sort of cellar, with an old, faded sign posted on the door. Whenever we walked in, there were always lots of men sitting around a table, and as soon as they saw my father, they would all stand up to greet him with reverence. One of them would make a gesture as if to take me into another room, but Papa opposed. "I want him to stay here. Don't worry. He's a little man; he'll behave himself," he'd say, looking at me with pride. I felt important next to him, silently drinking a glass of aranciata and eating coconut cookies.

Back then I was a very good kid, even my mom says so: "When you were little, you were an angel!" as though being good depended on the presence of my father.

In that cellar, badly lit by neon lights, almost everyone smoked, and the ashtrays were always full of cigarette butts. Some chewed on little green leaves, but my father didn't do either of those things—he didn't smoke, he didn't chew, he spoke with authority to those present and used difficult words, the kind that are hard for a kid to understand.

One night when we got home, my mom, hugging me, asked: "You smell like smoke. Where did he take you?"

I didn't respond, even though Papa was watching TV and couldn't hear us. It was supposed to be our secret. But later, while I was trying to fall asleep, I heard their voices coming from the living room: "You've kept me from participating in the liberation of our people! Let me go! There are still loyalists to the dictator—we have to annihilate them."

"War is not the answer. You have to stay with us, we're your family."

I didn't understand who the people he had to liberate were or even what annihilating someone means. Inside, I only hoped that Papa wouldn't leave and that he'd stay with us forever.

It's been many years since I've seen him. In the country where I was born, there's the civil war, and one day my father left us to go fight. He pulled on khaki pants and camouflage combat boots and put himself in command of an army, and the soldiers agreed to obey him, so long as he'd restore order for all.

The wise men didn't know how to get rid of the cruel beasts, so the people turned to two powerful magicians and rivals, Abow and Saykayeele.

"Do something!" they begged them. "Frightening monsters live in the river that Xiltir and Goole brought us."

Abow went to an enormous garas tree and, after having lifted it from the ground with a spell, commanded: "Go to the river, and crush all the crocodiles!"

Saykayeele went to a giant anthill and, after having lifted it from the ground, commanded: "Go and destroy all the crocodiles!"

The people waited along the riverbank to be freed from the terror, but when they saw the two magicians being followed by the tree and the giant anthill, they were even more frightened. The people feared the two new creatures more than they did the crocodiles.

"The garas tree and the anthill are much more dangerous than the beasts of the river," said Yabar, a man who knew how to speak to animals. "We'd better ask the magicians to interrupt their magic."

"Then who will protect you from those terrible animals? Remember that you were the ones to ask for our help!" the magicians admonished the people.

"I'll help you live alongside the crocodiles," Yabar offered himself, "whenever I am asked."

The people joyfully accepted his proposal, and Yabar was elected commander of the river and of all its creatures: his duty was to protect the people and livestock from the crocodiles. The two magicians accepted the villagers' wish, entrusted the two monsters to the commander, and gave the crocodiles an order: "From now on, you'll obey Yabar, otherwise you'll all be destroyed by the garas tree and the anthill." The crocodiles agreed to obey Yabar and went back to swimming in the river.

"And if the magicians had refused to bend to the will of the people or, even worse, if they couldn't stop the monsters, what would've happened to the river, the people, the crocodiles?" I ask.

Zia Rosa responds slowly. She seems to be searching for the most appropriate words while speaking: "If disproportionate, sometimes remedies are worse than evil."

"But are we sure that the crocodiles will obey Yabar, like the magicians instructed them to? And will he manage, if necessary, to frighten them with the garas tree and the anthill?"

"We must be very wise to exercise the power that is bestowed upon us. The crocodiles are a necessary evil, yet the river people can't live without water, so they elected the commander to help them govern it."

"Were the wise men and the magicians the ones to nominate the commander of the river, or was it all the people together?"

"The commander of the river proposed himself: 'I'll protect you from the crocodiles; elect me,' he said, and the people elected him because they believed his words. Yabar knows medicinal herbs and spells, he knows how to charm the crocodiles and get them to obey him, and he doesn't act in his own interest, but in that of the people."

It's seven o'clock. I didn't get much sleep. They brought me tea, toast, and jam for breakfast. There was an apple too. Later, the nurse will take me to another eye appointment.

I couldn't get through to my mother's phone last night. Zia Rosa says it's because there's no service in the mountains. She'll bring me what I need, I made her a list: T-shirts, shorts, slippers, toothbrush, toothpaste, and soup. Good thing she has our house keys. She comes early, she looks distressed. "I didn't sleep a wink last night."

She hands me a newspaper, I'd asked her to buy one for me. "Isn't it hard for you to read?"

"I just have to take a look at the local news," I reply.

"Since when do you care about local news? I thought you only concerned yourself with the world's biggest problems!" I smile, thankfully she quickly changes the subject.

She has a big cloth bag with her, and she mechanically repeats everything she'd put in it, but she'd forgotten the soap and is all torn up about it.

I stink. My nails are dirty. "It's because of the medicine," she justifies. "I'll go to the pharmacy downstairs and buy you some soap." I stop her, I'd rather she kept me company.

"It's early, they're probably still closed. Stay with me, I have an appointment soon. What time do you have to go to work?"

"I asked for some time off today, I'll go in later. When are they taking you to the eye doctor?"

"At eight, not for another hour or so. Let's go outside, I can't take any more of just lying in bed."

When I stand up I feel dizzy. I still have the IV needle stuck in my arm, a bandage keeps it in place. They're filling me with antibiotics and cortisone. Zia Rosa walks next to me. We look like the Fox and the Cat from Pinocchio, except that we truly are blind and crippled. We go out onto the balcony, the air is cool. I feel better immediately.

I sip the scorching hot tea. Zia Rosa brought coffee in a small thermos. She pours herself some. "What were you saying yesterday?"

"What was I saying? Ah, yes. That the choices you and Mama make are your own business, I'm not going to judge. You can even continue to keep your love lives secret if that suits you. But some things don't concern only you—do you understand what I mean? Sissi, for example, she's always known where her father was."

"It's a different story, Yabar, you know that."

"Of course. The problem is that Mama has always kept this very different story hidden from me."

I'm a little choked up. Zia Rosa grabs my hand.

"Have I ever told you how Sissi's father won me over?"

I shake my head.

"I was in university, in my third year of humanities. My father had died, and I was already living alone in Testaccio in his enormous house. Anyway, I was sitting in the hallway, waiting to go into the classroom, when this boy materialized out of nowhere. So pale, with his blond dreadlocks gathered up like a bird's nest. He hands me a piece of paper and sits down next to me. 'Ahh, finally!' he sighs.

"'Finally what?' I ask him.

"'I've only been back a month but can no longer stand seeing so many white people around.'

"I look at him, shocked.

"'Back from where?'

"'Mali,' he responds. 'Do you want to come?' he says, pointing at the flyer. It's an invitation to the concert of a Malian musician on Via di Monte Testaccio. It's even close to my house.

"'I think I would, actually.'

"Back then everything that pertained even distantly to Africa was an irresistible call to me. I made no distinction between countries, languages, colors—I was interested in all of it. I know, it's absurd, such indiscriminate attraction. I would read 'African dance class' and run straight to sign up. If I wanted to go out to dinner with friends, without a doubt the Ethiopian restaurant was my first choice. One time I even went to Milan on my own for the African cinema festival. You know, when my father and his sister—the one who ended up raising me—were still alive, they never let me express my need for Africa. I didn't even know my own mother, practically. Everything having to do with her was taboo. A void and a myth at the same time."

"And was that when you started buying all those African amulets and fabrics?"

"Exactly, all those 'knickknacks,' as your mom calls them, they filled me with warmth. It was like cultivating a part of me that I hadn't had access to before.

"But let's get back to Max, Sissi's father. That man was capable of building a house from the ground up. He'd learned the trade from his father, who'd worked as a foreman all over Africa. Leaving behind Bergamo, his birth city, he'd gone to Nigeria with his wife and son. Can you imagine? Max must have been a year old at the time. Just think what an effect he must've had on the other children with all that yellow hair. His father was the restless type. They moved continuously: Nigeria, Ivory Coast, Senegal, Kenya, Tanzania. He himself seemed to have lost count of the places he'd lived. And it's not like they settled in the cities—ah, no!—they lived in small villages. Often they were the only

Europeans for kilometers around. At a certain point his mother got fed up with wandering, with Africa, with her husband, and she ditched them. Maybe that's why Max was so uncivilized. But I told you—as a construction worker, electrician, or plumber, he was a magician. When I was pregnant with Sissi, we threw out all the heavy heirloom furniture, tore down partitions, rewired the electrical system. Yes, the lighting, the most important thing. The house we live in, as you see it today, is in large part his handiwork. I couldn't do any heavy lifting because of the pregnancy, but I helped him paint, add the finishing touches, set up Sissi's little room. On breaks, we allowed ourselves a snack of fruit or raw vegetables: Max was very concerned about my nutrition. We were building a future together, and we felt very precarious and poetic."

When Zia Rosa tells a story, she sometimes loses herself in all the memories.

"And then you met up at the African music concert?" I ask so she'll get to the point.

"Yes—such a wonderful evening. Max knew everyone and never left my side. He introduced me to his friends as if we'd known each other forever. That's what it's like, you know, at the beginning. When you fall in love, I mean. It's as if you and the other person had always known each other. Max organized concerts, he brought important musicians to Rome. Africans and others from the diaspora. Sissi inherited her love of music from him. He also took care of the food. He employed a Senegalese woman capable of cooking delicacies for an army. He was even talented at plate presentation. He'd decorate them, arrange the food in an elegant way. Right away he asked me to help him. There was a lot of work to be done, and I would've gotten involved even if he hadn't asked me to. Those were great years."

"When is it that things changed?"

"When Sissi was born. I could no longer only attend to Max, keep up with his every project. I'd been awarded a position at the library. We needed a salary we could count on. That man, many great ideas, but then what? And in any case, Sissi took up a lot of my energy. Most of all those first few years."

"I'm sure he understood. I like Max. From the few times we've met."

"Of course you like him. What do you know? If he'd only just been able to admit that he didn't need a wife but a nanny, it would've ended differently. Instead, he told me he could no longer stand the winters and that he wanted to go home. Who even knows which home he was talking about?"

"Zia, know what I think? The truth is you and Mama are too proud and always want to have it your own way."

"What do you mean?"

"The way things are going, Sissi will never find a boyfriend. She's become like the two of you—men must be perfect to be good enough for you. To know about Africa, love music, study like nerds, run, swim, and I don't know how many other things."

Zia Rosa bursts out laughing.

"I'll admit it, both Zahra and I have a hard time trusting people. What can you do? As for Sissi, if I were you, I really wouldn't worry. She'll find a boyfriend, her time will come. And you'll be jealous like every other self-respecting older brother."

Many years ago, my mom brought me to see a movie where Will Smith plays the part of the intergalactic agent. I walked out of the theater enthusiastic—finally I had a hero who was not only clever and kind but had black skin like mine. I had to have a Willie action figure, as Agent J, and after an exhausting search, Mama granted my wish. One afternoon, she came back from work with a surprise: she'd been at Rocco Balocco, the best-supplied toy store in the neighborhood, and she'd found one! Even though he wasn't wearing a black jacket, tie, and pants like in the movie, but some sort of purple tracksuit with a built-in backpack, I was still happy. A knowing look between us was enough to realize what we had to do. My mom helped me saw off the action figure's head, and we used Super Attak to glue it to the naked body of an extremely muscular warrior, which I then colored with a brown permanent marker, so that he'd have the same color skin as my hero. Mama set about sewing an entire wardrobe for Willie. The first outfit she made identical to the one in the movie: she used some leftover black satin and the white part was from a napkin. Then there was the astronaut suit—we cut a ball of silver-colored plastic to make the helmet and used the green net from the lemon packaging to sew part of the suit. It was a difficult task because my Willie was only ten centimeters tall. The last outfit I remember was the soldier one. For that we used the burlap of a Thai rice package and the little leather square of its label.

I was always holding Willie in my hand or in my pocket—I couldn't separate myself from him. If someone in class took him from me, I made a scene: I'd push my desk and tear out paper from my notebook. Even at the table during lunch and dinner I wanted him nearby, and when I went to bed, he slept with me. My teacher would get mad, she said I was distracted. And even my mom, after a period of initial tolerance, started telling me I was overdoing it.

The day my teacher confiscated him, saying that he would stay on top of the cabinet until I learned to pay attention during class, I went home in a panic. I couldn't think about anything else—until I got an idea.

In no time at all I'd make a fake Will Smith, painting him brown and constructing his clothes with crepe paper. The plan was so exciting, I decided to involve Sissi, who not only helped me disguise the fake Willie but was essential in the risky undertaking of his substitution. Only she could understand why that action figure was so important to me.

The next morning, we got to school really early, before my teacher and classmates and, while she held a chair still, I climbed up onto the cabinet to retrieve Willie and substitute him with our creation.

It all went smoothly, and we were so excited that for days we couldn't stop talking about our secret mission. I no longer dared to pull out the true Willie, who continued to be my inseparable companion for another couple years until the terrible day I lost him forever.

At the time, Zia Rosa was running daily along the river, and on the rare occasions in which Sissi's father was in town between one trip and another, he'd bring us down to that very same trail for a bike ride.

There's a point along the river, near Castel Sant'Angelo, where the water slows and forms an island near one bank. We used to love stopping there to watch the nutrias, they look like beavers with the tail of a mouse. There were big ones and baby ones. We'd throw them bread crumbs, and they competed for them, swimming in the shallow water. Maybe they'd been the ones to build that mountain of dirt, like beavers do with dams. The little island was clearly their home. Max thought they were gross, he said they looked like enormous rats with those big teeth and long, slimy tails, but Sissi always had a great time and took pictures of them with her camera.

That fateful day, we had gone down by the river for one of our bike rides. Willie was dressed in the soldier uniform, the one Mama had sewn with the burlap. He was attached to my handlebars—I'd tied him down with twine so he'd remain stable and could experience the adventure too. It was very windy—the trail was invaded by branches, sycamore leaves, pine needles, and our bicycles bounced over them, *tu-tum, tu-tum*.

Some stringy debris had been left caught in the trees after the last flooding, it hung down like long, gray beards. It was the first time I'd noticed it, it gave the river a gloomy and solemn feel. It reminded me of the magic of Mama and Zia Rosa's fable, and I wouldn't have been surprised if crocodiles appeared.

Suddenly a protruding branch struck the handlebars of my bicycle, hitting Willie directly. In the fall, his head detached from his body and rolled toward the river. I screeched to a halt to avoid the worst, but the next thing I knew the water had swallowed everything: the broken branch and Willie's head. Sissi knew how dramatic the moment was for me, and she got off her bike to retrieve the headless body. I didn't have the courage to hold or look at it. I was so upset, I couldn't even talk. Meanwhile, Max also stopped a little further ahead and did a U-turn to come back and join us.

Sissi told him: "He's crying because his Willie lost his head." And they both tried to console me. While Sissi stood still with Willie's body in her hands, Max silently rolled a cigarette. Neither of them dared to say: "We'll find a new head for your Willie." Both, in fact, knew well that Willie could only have one head and it had rolled into the river.

When we got back home, right before dinner, I heard Mama whisper to Zia Rosa: "Finally, we're free of it!"

8

ZIA ROSA RUSHES over to me. She'd waited outside for the duration of the appointment.

"We don't know if he'll recover vision in his right eye," Doctor Bandanna tells her. "There's a hole in the macula, the most sensitive part of the retina. Everything depends on how the internal hematoma reabsorbs and how it manages to heal."

"What are the odds?"

"Signora, it's too early to make any predictions. He could go back to seeing as before, or he could stay like this."

"As in practically blind out of one eye?"

"Correct."

Zia Rosa starts visibly sweating again.

"Get him to tell you what happened," the doctor adds while closing the door behind him. Before Zia Rosa has time to say even a single word, a new patient has already come in.

She sits down, her strength drained.

"You see what they're like?" I comment, seated in the wheelchair. "They announce your ill-fated future and then ciao, on to the next. What does it matter to them anyway?"

"What else can they do?" she sighs.

"Yeah, but did you see all the other patients?" I add, lowering my voice. "All old people. It's an entirely different thing."

"He should feel sadder because you're young?"

"I'd say so."

"He doesn't have time to feel pity. Now you—why don't you tell me what really happened?"

"I did. I fell."

"If that's what you want to call it, it's your business. You can take it up with your mother." Zia Rosa leans into the wheelchair, pushing it with her body weight. "Look, I'm going to bring you back upstairs now, I have to go to work. Zahra will be home in a couple days, but I'm sure she'll call us before then. Would you like to hear from Sissi?"

"No. I mean, I'd like to, but let her enjoy her vacation. How's it all going?"

"She's happy. She'd been wanting to go to England to improve her English for a while now, and she's having a good time there. She likes her host family. She's sharing a room with a French girl. They always place you with someone from a different nationality so you're forced to speak in English."

"And she's speaking it?"

"Of course. They have four hours of class in the morning, and in the afternoon they can choose between tennis, horseback riding, and other sports. They also do cultural trips, they go visit museums and monuments."

"Where is it that she went, exactly?"

"Lowestoft, in Suffolk, on the eastern coast."

"When is she coming back?"

"In a week."

"Well, there you go. Better not tell her anything. For all she knows I shouldn't even be in Rome. Even though we had a fight, she'd still be sorry to hear I'm in the hospital, probably. Or do you think she couldn't care less?"

"Don't be silly, of course she'd care! Hey—what about the Sybarite?"

"I'll call him when you leave."

The Sybarite is my best friend. We've known each other since we were in the same elementary school class, and we've stayed close all these years. The Sybarite is giant and super strong; that's how he's always been. He wears an earring that makes him look like a pirate. In fact, people get scared when they see him, but he wouldn't hurt a fly. He's loyal and very sensitive—when he was little, he cried a lot because no one ever believed him. For example, that time Mama brought us to the Botanical Garden in Trastevere, the man in the ticket booth asked how old he was, and when he said seven, the man thought it was a scam to get in free. Thankfully Mama was there as a witness. Despite his teary eyes, we had a blast fishing for tadpoles in the pond, hiding in the bamboo, climbing in the rocky garden, and reading the nameplates of the most mysterious plants, like the Montezuma cypress, the Caucasian wingnut, the Assyrian plum, and the cloud tree—strange names I still remember.

I'd go over to the Sybarite's house often and, sometimes, when she felt like it, Sissi would come too. My friend and I kept to ourselves, while she, because she loved little children, took care of the Sybarite's little brother, whose name is Valerio and who was only a year old at the time. They would toddle around the house hand in hand, she'd explain everything to him, she was already like a teacher—do this, don't do that. She taught him words, and sometimes she even wanted to change his diaper—who had the heart to explain to her that he wasn't a doll? Zia Rosa used to say that she would've liked to give Sissi a little brother or sister, but sadly they never arrived, and besides, by that time she and Max had been broken up for a while. Still, Sissi had gotten lucky just the same because right when she was no longer hoping for it, I came along, and it's even more fun to have a brother your age.

You could say Sissi and the Sybarite met thanks to me, but then became close friends on their own a couple years later when they began studying music right across the street from our old middle school. With time, music became a full-blown mania for them both: Sissi played the piano and tried to imitate the singers on MTV, while the Sybarite had to practice his saxophone every day, come hell or high water. A few times they attempted to convince me to try it with them, but I've never wanted anything to do with playing a musical instrument.

I'm lucky to have a friend like the Sybarite—he's pulled me out of trouble a million times because I'm always ready to start fights with people. I don't know why, but I never mind my own business. I clench my fists at even a hint of provocation, but no one steps forward when the Sybarite's with me.

Not a day goes by that we don't see each other at his house or at mine. If we're going out, he's the one who comes to get me. He leans on the buzzer—it's an obsession, he demands a response, he doesn't know how to wait—and I yell back: "I'm coming, cut it out!"

One day, he came over with Sissi and wouldn't take his finger off the buzzer—same scene as always. I was taking a shower and had to get out still wet. It was winter, and I almost froze. I opened the door, and they sat down to wait for me in the living room while I went back into my wonderful, boiling-hot shower with Pino Silvestre bodywash, which has always been my favorite.

Once I finished, I put on clothes and cologne at my leisure, then found them sprawled out on the couch, looking annoyed. That's when my friend said: "You're such a sybarite."

Neither Sissi nor I knew the meaning of that word, and we burst out laughing. Right away Sissi grabbed a dictionary because she's Miss Meticulous and when she hears a word she doesn't know, she rushes to look it up. Then she read the definition out loud: "Sybarite—from Sybaris, an ancient Greek city, used to describe someone who is lazy and loves luxury."

We haven't had any doubts since that day: "Sybarite" became our friend's nickname even though he's the exact opposite of a sybarite.

It's not like he's always had to be at my beck and call—I've also had to wait for him many times! Often I'd end up going over to visit without any warning just because I wanted to see him. Maybe he'd be practicing the saxophone, so I'd walk around the neighborhood, waiting for him to finish.

The Sybarite lives in the Ostiense neighborhood too, in a building shaped like a ring with a big courtyard in the middle. From the windows hangs laundry that's covered with plastic when it rains, and there are two giant flowerbeds with rose-bushes and dwarf palms that children and cats run around in.

One afternoon, while I was waiting for him to let me in, an old lady coming out of the building asked me: "Are you the friend of the guy with the trumpet?" And because I replied, "No, I don't know who that is," she got irritated and said: "Are you kidding me? I always see you two together!"

"You see me with the saxophone guy, not the trumpet guy," I clarified.

"Trumpet and saxophone are the same thing to me. You have to tell him to stop. Enough is enough!"

"You're telling me! Anyway—it's music, it's not just noise!"

The woman felt even more mocked and, raising up her umbrella (I don't know why certain old ladies always carry an umbrella with them even when it's sunny out), she grumbled: "You're a very rude boy! I'll show you music!" I tried to explain that I was on her side when it came to the saxophone, but at that point she was no longer listening to me, but walking away muttering.

I went in the main door and started climbing two stairs at a time because there's no elevator and my friend lives on the top floor. His room is in the shed on the building's rooftop that was made to house a water tank, and it's surrounded by beautiful plants: a fragrant wisteria, a lemon tree, a few papyruses, and a row of pots with geraniums. The Sybarite waters them every day, with a gentleness unusual for someone of his size. We used to call that open-air space our secret garden, and the shed was the playroom.

"What are you doing here at this hour?" he asked, poking his head out.

"I came to chat." The Sybarite held the door open only a crack and didn't show the slightest intention of letting me in.

"I'm practicing—you know I'm always busy at this time. Come back in a bit."

"I'll just stay here and listen to you."

"But you hate music!"

"I can always change my mind."

"Listening to arpeggios isn't fun."

"Pretend I'm not here."

"I can't, Yabar, and anyway, it won't take long before you blurt out one of your lines."

"No, I won't, I promise. But tell me one thing—don't you get bored doing the same exercises every single day?"

"Exactly, there you go."

"Okay, actually, I came to tell you that the woman from the fourth floor wants you to stop."

"I know. She tells me every day."

"Oh, and you just blow it off? Is that the kind of respect you show little old ladies?"

"Yabar, knock it off and let me practice a little longer. Why don't you go take a walk?"

"All right, I'll see you in about an hour."

Having left the courtyard, I headed toward Lungotevere Testaccio. I'd gone that route so many times I knew it by heart: the former slaughterhouse at one end, the old river port at the other, and, almost halfway, a very strange fountain in the shape of a sarcophagus where water gushes out from the head of a lion. It's right in front of Cattaneo, the technical school where I would've gone if only Sissi hadn't gotten it into her head that I wasn't cut out for vocational schools.

I was very thirsty, so I stopped for a drink. I had to wait at least another half hour before going back to the Sybarite, so I sat down on a short pillar nearby to roll myself a cigarette. I was just quietly smoking there, minding my own business, when suddenly I saw a woman appear. From far away she looked gorgeous. She was wearing a blue veil like a poncho, the sleeves so wide they were like wings in the wind.

She was singing in a gloomy, mournful voice and advancing, pointing at me with her finger. By now she was close enough to tell that she was completely naked under the veil and the thing I'd thought was a necklace was, in reality, a rope with which she was towing some sort of cart packed full of bags. Her flabby body stank of pee and filth like all hobos. Once she reached the fountain, she freed herself from the noose, pulled out a plastic bottle with the top cut off, and began filling it, then emptying it out on herself. The scene was exactly how I'd imagined Stinky washing himself in the clear water of the spring. I was frozen with fear and couldn't take my eyes off her—she had translucent skin, little, wrinkled breasts, and a bush of hair between her legs. She didn't seem to notice me, so I, taking advantage of the fact that I was behind her, stood up to leave. I didn't even have the time to take two steps when, abruptly stopping her bath, she gestured to me that she wanted a cigarette.

I, more out of fear than kindness, pulled out a paper and a bit of tobacco. She stared at me with two wide-open, opaque eyes like those of crazy people, and since I wasn't rolling the cigarette very quickly, both to buy some time and to fortify myself, I asked her: "What's the reason for all those bags?"

She looked at me with a dumbfounded expression, as if I were the crazy one, and then, without replying, began searching for something in her pile of trash. Finally, after having rummaged around for a while in her luggage, she pulled out a disgusting bag. Just the idea of touching it made me cringe but, seeing as she wouldn't otherwise take the cigarette and was just standing there, I had to accept it. The woman smiled at me with all her rotten teeth, as though she'd given me who knows what gift, then she put the cigarette between her lips and waited for me to light it. My hands shook so much, I wasted many matches before succeeding. The woman inhaled, all satisfied, and smoked standing up as straight as an arrow, the blue veil stuck to her body. Then she went back to ignoring me, again singing to the ghosts with her hoarse voice, and I took the opportunity to walk away. Every so often I turned back to see if she were still watching me because I couldn't wait to throw the bag in the trash and tell the Sybarite everything.

My phone rings, it's my mother again. I'll have to pick up sooner or later. I squeeze it, the light is flashing. I don't feel like hearing her yell. Usually I put up with it. I don't rebel. She instilled her principles in me. Respect your father and mother. But now it's different. I discovered the truth, the one she'd kept hidden from me.

The Sybarite is on his way, I'll use that as an excuse. I don't want to talk to her for more than five minutes. I press the green button and hold the phone away from my ear. There, I knew it: "Did you want to give me a heart attack? I can't even take a vacation—I go back down to the valley and find an avalanche of messages. How did you end up in the hospital?"

I stay silent.

"Are you there? Yabar! Can you hear me? What'd you do to your eye? Waryaa! Say something!"

"Yes, Mama. Calm down, it's nothing!"

"Why are you in Rome when you're supposed to be in London?"

"You know why."

I'm done being the respectful son I used to be. My vision is cloudy, my head hurts.

"What am I supposed to know, exactly?"

I fling my phone to the floor. At least now it'll stop ringing. It breaks into three pieces—battery to one side, keyboard and cover to the other. Thankfully there's no one else out here on the balcony. It's dinnertime for the patients. But I'm not hungry, the smell of food makes me nauseous.

After a while, the Sybarite arrives. He'd followed my directions.

"Yabar, it took me ages to find you, and your phone's disconnected! I brought you some gelato, but by now it'll be all melted."

He sees my phone on the ground.

"What happened?"

"Nothing, it was my mom."

He hugs me and sits down. The Sybarite isn't much of a talker. He knows how to listen and respond in a sensible way. In my family, instead, everyone talks too much. Mama, Zia Rosa, and Sissi. They mess with your head.

The gelato is in fact almost completely liquid.

"Thanks for the gesture. But next time maybe it'd be better if you brought me cigarettes."

"You'd asked for them, but I thought you were joking. I didn't think you could smoke in the hospital."

"Out here you can."

"I brought you these too," he adds, taking two books out of his backpack, *Corto Maltese* comics and something else.

"Thank you, but I can't read with just one eye."

"I'm sorry." He's embarrassed. "If only I'd gotten one thing right. Melted gelato and books you can't read!"

"Don't worry about it. What's that book called?"

"*A Defeat of Intelligence. Italy and Somalia.*"

"A relaxing read, in other words."

There's an unlimited supply of essays and historical novels at the Sybarite's house. His father lets us raid it on the condition that the books are always put back in their places. Even Sissi tries to read them every so often, but she never gets past the first twenty pages—she likes myths better, and romantic stories. "I understand the Sybarite because he's a nerd, but you, how can you wade through these bricks? You know, studying is much simpler!"

The Sybarite gathers the pieces of my phone scattered across the ground. "Want me to fix it for you?"

"As long as you keep it turned off."

I page through the book he brought me. "I bet it's interesting," I say. I don't feel like diving straight into what happened. My friend goes along with me.

"It's about the relationship between Somalia and Italy from the fifties to 1993."

"The history of Somalia is tied so closely to Italy's. But it's as if no one knows. Think about it. Even classes at the Somali university were in Italian. Mama told me that to attend them the students first had to do a preparatory semester to learn the language."

"The colonial language. One time you told me your father studied military cartography and topography at the University of Florence. That stuck with me."

"Papa was a little older than Mama. He already spoke Italian. Remember, though, that education was Somalized in the seventies, so Mama belongs to the first generation that did school in its mother tongue."

"Didn't she study dental hygiene?"

"Something like that. The policy was to train more paramedics. And soldiers, I'm afraid."

"We've seen the result. Fifteen years of war."

"And who knows how much longer it'll last."

"In any case, I really can't picture your mother with a soldier . . . how did they meet when they belonged to such different worlds?"

"I think they already knew each other. My father had just come back from Italy. He had a younger sister who, from what I've understood, studied with Mama. But I've never met her. I only know the story. I heard Mama telling it to Zia Rosa. You know what they're like. One anecdote leads to another—they're always talking to each other about the past."

"It can't hurt. That's why you know a bunch of things."

"Only about a few topics."

"Like the history of Somalia. Makes sense to me."

"The problem is that my personal history . . . that's something I can't find in the books."

"Yeah . . . but anyway, what's the story about your father's sister that you heard being told?"

"Oh, right. It's really funny. This aunt of mine on my father's side gets a zero on an exam in university. Mama says they couldn't make sense of it because she was one of the best students. So they go talk to the professor—who was Italian—and this guy explains that he had to throw out her test because she'd copied."

"How was he able to prove it?"

"Apparently she'd responded with sentences that were identical to the ones in the book. So my father's sister asks him to give her a second chance. My mother insists on her behalf. But the professor won't hear of it, he can't give her special treatment. And that's how my father comes into play. He was the older brother, just back from Italy—he had more credibility."

"And he managed to convince him?"

"Of course. So my aunt took the exam again, while my parents—who at the time weren't yet married—waited for her outside. And to the professor's great surprise, again the answers seemed to be copied straight from the book."

"But he'd monitored her, right?"

"Yes, the entire time. So my father explains to the Italian professor that Somalis begin exercising their memory when they're children, they even memorize texts they don't understand, like the Koran, or their family trees—in fact, they're all capable of going back generations. What's an ordinary book in comparison? Mama was very impressed by his reasoning, and so they began seeing each other . . . it's just a pity that then the whole thing with the family tree turned out to be so damaging. For years, Somalis have been fighting against each other in the name of phantom affiliations."

"You'll have to explain that to me sooner or later. Guess what? I don't even know the names of my great-grandparents! My parents have never told me them."

"I'm not surprised! Have they already left for vacation, or are they still around?"

"No, I'm the only one here in Rome."

9

THE SYBARITE ALWAYS cooks in his mom's apron. It really cracks me up when he puts it on, he says that all chefs use them and they also wear a hat on their heads so hair doesn't fall into the food. He carefully prepares the sauce—he even uses a mezzaluna knife to chop up scallions, carrots, and celery very finely, then lightly sautés it all in olive oil. When you start to smell the aroma, he pours in a can of finely chopped tomatoes and, in the meantime, puts the water on to boil.

I love watching the Sybarite while he's at the stove—it's funny how serious he is. He adds a bit of milk and a triangle of butter to the sauce and declares: "This cuts the acidity of the tomato," as if I knew anything about acidity or about tomatoes.

One evening, it was just the two of us at his house, and we decided to eat dinner early. I was enjoying it all on the building's rooftop—the sweet scent of wisteria, the delicious spaghetti—but the Sybarite kept reminding me that we had to hurry up, just two short hours and the concert would be starting.

He was, in fact, supposed to play with his band at Cantiere, and Sissi would be singing a song she'd written herself, for the first time. Cantiere is the centro sociale I'd been to with Stella

Ricorsi, the one on the cross street in front of Piazza Gioachino Belli, where there's a statue of the poet supporting himself with a black iron cane because the original ebony one had been stolen from him repeatedly.

I was happy to go, even though I couldn't say I loved concerts, and I practically hadn't seen Sissi since the day with the pepper spray.

The problem with the four of them—Mama, Zia Rosa, Sissi, the Sybarite—is that they're completely obsessed with music. I, instead, think that to be able to concentrate it's important to sit in silence every so often. Music changes things in your head, the way you see and feel them. Sissi, for example, always runs with headphones. It's beautiful to watch her run: the wind lifts the leaves, and she seems to drift alongside the river as soft as a cloud. One time, I dared to ask her: "Sissi, can you even hear the wind? Can you hear the river and the leaves?" But she heard none of it, all she could hear was the music in her ears. The Sybarite claims that everyone has his or her own music and I simply have to find the one that suits me. Said in that way, it seems to me like a pretty abstract concept, but maybe he's right.

The river road was already flooded with traffic, and the Sybarite walked quickly in front of me with the saxophone on his back. Once we got to Cantiere, I left, promising him I'd be back soon—after a short walk and a cigarette. I wanted to spare myself from seeing Sissi before the show. I headed toward Tiber Island, to the corner right before the bridge with the kiosk that makes my favorite shaved ice.

In the summer, Lungotevere fills up with stands and stages. People walk along and no longer smell only the odor of algae and swamp because the kiosks sell french fries, fried fish, drinks, and fresh fruit.

It was starting to get dark out, and there was a long line for shaved ice. I didn't feel like waiting in line, so I sat down on a chair nearby to see if it would eventually shorten. Meanwhile, I lit another cigarette and watched the guy scraping the ice; he must have some nice muscles from all that going back and forth with the blade. From the slab of ice, many little chips broke off and sparkled all different colors, a boy filled the cups, and a woman added syrups and pieces of dried or fresh fruit to it, depending on taste.

I was so concentrated on watching his movements and counting the people in line that I didn't realize that at least half an hour must've gone by. Someone next to me looked at the time on their cell phone and, all of a sudden, seeing the bright numbers, I was filled with anxiety, as though the show had ended without me. So I started running and, seeing as I'd just smoked the umpteenth cigarette, began coughing like an old man. By that point, there were a lot of people in front of the centro sociale and, ironically, not only had I not gotten the shaved ice I'd wanted, I now had to stand in another line.

At the entrance was a big black guy who looked like a gorilla dressed as a penguin. When it was my turn, I told him that I'd come earlier with my friends, but had decided to wait outside so as not to bother them while they rehearsed.

He asked me: "Who are your friends?" and I didn't say the Sybarite's name, but Sissi's—I was certain that the name of the singer would seem more impressive.

Mr. Fancy Pants looked at a list and, not seeing my name, spoke into his walkie-talkie, and then to me: "Wait here."

On the centro sociale's main door, framed by the purple bougainvillea, was a poster with a list of the groups performing that night and, right next to it, a board with various colored flyers. Among them, there was one definitely drawn by Sissi. In fact, in the middle of this flyer was a face encircled by spiderwebs and some text announcing that Sam and His Pietrini would be playing that evening with a special guest: Spider Hair, afroitalian singer-songwriter. I wanted to laugh—Sissi sure had a lot of courage and, as far as names go, even the Sybarite and his friend Samuele weren't joking around.

Tincaaro, the queen of the giants, appeared every now and then in the book of Somali fables that Zia Rosa read to us. There wasn't much written on her, but the few lines about the giants of the clouds who at one point commanded all of Somalia, softened the earth with butter, and dug springs with their own hands were enough to conquer Sissi's imagination.

I was out there waiting when I saw a figure appear behind the guy with the walkie-talkie. Big hair and wearing a silver jumpsuit that made her look as slender as a slipstream.

The man, stationary at the door, asked her: "Should we let this one in?"

Sissi looked me in the eye, then replied: "He's not my friend." And she turned around without looking at me again.

It's just that, seeing her done up in such a way, a sort of snicker slipped out. It's a problem, I'm unable to restrain myself. What can I do? Sissi says it happens to me because I never take anything seriously, so I end up always ruining the important moments.

I tried to grab her arm, but in response she wriggled away, screaming at me: "You hate music and don't understand my songs, I'd rather die than have you listen to me."

The bouncer placed his huge hand on my chest and asked: "You hear her?" and now he was the one snickering, while Sissi walked away, sparkling in the dark like a flame.

10

ACCORDING TO A folktale, Castel Sant'Angelo owes its name to a vision. It seems, in fact, that very, very long ago, back when the plague was devastating the Romans, the pope saw an angel sheathe his fiery sword on top of the fortress—a sign that the terrible epidemic had ceased.

On the banks of the Tiber, for a few years now, you can embark on riverboats and admire Rome while navigating its waters. One of the landings is located near the Sant'Angelo Bridge, a floating platform enameled white. Ever since this service began, I've dreamed of going on board one of those boats.

"You've never made much of an effort!" the Sybarite always jokes. He doesn't believe that all the times I've tried it just didn't work out. Like the time I was heading home on my bike. I'll take a detour, I told myself. Let's see whether this time I manage to make my wish come true. When I arrived at the platform, I found the gangway raised and the riverboat anchored to the opposite bank.

The sun was beginning to go down, and there were seagulls everywhere, as though they were the angels of the castle. They sat motionless in a row above the arches, somewhat like the statues on the bridge. I don't know what got into me, but I took a running start and jumped onto the platform to make them fly away. Hearing the big thud, a man looked over at me, all surprised. I think he lived there nearby, maybe under the bridge. Seeing the birds suspended midair, he began laughing and threw fistfuls of bread up into the air.

The seagulls flew around him, and the man made strange gestures with his hands, as though he had the power to speak to birds. Dazed, I stood there watching him for a while and hoping, maybe subconsciously, for a riverboat in transit.

When Sissi didn't want to let me into the centro sociale, I felt the same way I had that time on the platform: I thought I had a plan and instead suddenly found myself alone with nothing to do.

The Sybarite examines me, puzzled: "Look, I just thought you'd changed your mind that night, that you'd gone off on your own free will. What do you think? It's not like Sissi told me she didn't let you in."

"But it never occurred to you to look for me? I was right outside waiting for you to come get me."

"I called you loads of times, you know that. Why didn't you pick up?"

"I didn't get any calls from you."

The Sybarite snorts, he knows me too well to fall into one of my traps. "Yabar, I had a show, I had to rehearse, I was tense. You need to stop trusting that things will happen because other people take initiative for you . . . you, too, have responsibilities. Sissi's right."

There are things my two closest friends will never truly understand—neither of them has bad habits—no smoking, no alcohol, no swear words; they follow the rules, do their homework, get to school on time.

"You have to find the secret of self-restraint on your own," Zia Rosa's always telling me. "You need to learn how to control your emotions, the outbursts of rage. And, when necessary, to withstand the pain. Good and evil are connected, as the fable with the commander shows us. Do you think it's a coincidence that the people decide to live alongside the crocodiles rather than giving up the water, and that they appoint the commander to govern the life of the river?"

I fail to stifle a sigh: "I might lose the use of my eye." This surprises the Sybarite, he says nothing. "You understand what the doctor told me? He doesn't know if I'll ever go back to seeing out of this eye again."

"You aren't going to lose your eye, Yabar. Try to be optimistic."

I'd missed the Sybarite, and I'm only realizing that now. More than a month has passed since the day of the concert. That night, after the bouncer told me to leave, I'd started smoking like crazy, one cigarette after the other. But even that wasn't enough to calm me down and, since I didn't know who to take it out on, I started kicking the wall. It was dark, and people didn't seem to notice me and my outburst until a guy separated from his group and came toward me. I immediately stopped—a bit out of embarrassment, a bit out of curiosity—and nodded hello. He had his hair divided into thick braids—in the semidarkness, his head looked like a sea urchin—and oblique eyes circled in black.

"Got a light?" he asked, then he introduced himself. His name was Ghiorghis; he must've been about ten years older than me.

Hearing his name, I was reminded of a painting Zia Rosa had and was very proud of. One of her Ethiopian friends had given it to her, and it depicted San Giorgio—Ghiorghis in their language—killing the dragon. The saint was very important for the Ethiopians, and as the legend goes, he'd killed the dragon because it was tormenting the inhabitants of a city called Selem, thus restoring peace among the people. Ghiorghis's face, upon closer look, was the spitting image of the saint's—in the painting his eyes are so big and bright they shine in the dark.

After having lit his cigarette, he looked at me with a concerned expression and, placing his hand on my shoulder, asked: "All good, brother?"

I was still angry about being left outside the centro sociale, so—partly to surprise him, partly to provoke him—I responded: "Why are you calling me brother when you don't even know me?"

Ghiorghis first stared at me, incredulous, then burst out laughing and waved his friends over. Some had dreadlocks, others shaved heads, still others were wearing hats with green, red, yellow, and black stripes—the colors of Rastas.

"Little brother, what happened to you?" another guy asked me while everyone gathered around. They all had black hands, and they seemed to have one voice that came out of their eyes.

I repeated: "Why are you calling me brother when you don't even know me?" And they, like Ghiorghis, also burst out laughing as if I'd said the strangest thing ever.

"What do you mean why? Where are you from, little dude? Who do you think you are?" said one with a certain defiance, after which Ghiorghis signaled for everyone to move away.

He was wearing a white short-sleeved shirt, rather tight, and an African necklace with colored beads. He was shorter than me but, being older, intimidated me.

"I'm sorry," I told him. "My friends just ditched me. And, by the way, I can't stand it when people ask me where I'm from."

Hearing these words, Ghiorghis smiled at me and sat down on a parked moped. "I know it can be annoying, but between us it's completely different."

It wasn't very clear to me what he meant by "between us" and, without my even asking, Ghiorghis explained that for him "between us" means that "you don't have to play any part, you can be yourself, while everyone else has certain expectations. If you go to a centro sociale, for example, they expect you to be someone who does more drugs than other people; if you go to a church, you must need something. All fabrications that missionaries, colonizers, and anthropologists came up with."

I really liked the word "fabrications" but still didn't understand—in fact, for me "between us" meant between Sissi, the Sybarite, and our families. Nothing could divide us, even though in that moment they were performing inside the centro sociale and I was outside.

Thinking about my two friends, I got choked up again and, in an almost angry voice, said to the guy: "All right, but what does this have to do with the inevitable question? Why do people always have to ask you where you're from and don't just mind their own business?"

Instead of losing patience, Ghiorghis began telling me a story from when he was a boy.

He was thirteen and was going to school in the Città dei Ragazzi, where he had an Italian American gym teacher. All the kids admired him and hung around him. One day, the teacher asked Ghiorghis: "Where are you from?"

"Ethiopia," he simply said.

Not happy with the answer, the Italian American pressed him again: "Where were you born?" and when he heard that Ghiorghis was born in Rome, he flipped out. He inundated Ghiorghis with a flood of words, a mix of American English and Campania dialect, telling him that he was Italian, not Ethiopian, because Italy was where he was born, received his first maternal caresses, made his first friends, attended school. Ghiorghis emphasized this word, "caresses," because his teacher had kept repeating it, pronouncing it in a strange way, rolling his r for twice as long.

"Then and there, it didn't seem like anything important . . . but over the years," Ghiorghis went on, "I've really reflected on that story—I might even say it's become my favorite parable."

Ghiorghis wasn't yet done with his reasoning. He still wanted to tell me how recently he'd happened to accompany a friend to look for a summer job at Caritas, where he'd met the priest on duty. The man had looked at him sympathetically and—guess what?—asked him: "Where are you from?"

"From Rome," Ghiorghis responded.

But the priest had persisted: "Ethiopian, Eritrean?"

"My parents are Ethiopian."

To this the guy had commented disapprovingly: "I don't care for your denial."

"Can you believe it?" Ghiorghis repeated, shaking his curly head—how dare he say he was rejecting his own origins? That he was denying being Ethiopian? The Italian American gym teacher had explained that your place is where you have ties, friends, it's where you know the streets and the smells.

I completely agreed with him about this, but there was still something that didn't make sense to me, so I asked: "If that's what you think, why did you choose friends who all look like you?"

Ghiorghis seemed to be enjoying himself again: "You're a tough nut to crack, you know?" And he gave me a slap on the back. "When I was your age more or less, I'd already been hanging out at the legendary Big Burger in Piazzale Flaminio for a few years. That's where my crew gathered. Well, actually, that's where almost all the black kids of Rome gathered. That piazza was the only place we felt was ours—we were free to say whatever we wanted, we weren't forced to play any part. We stopped being what other people saw us as, we were no longer 'the beggar,' 'the junkie,' 'the loser,' 'the well-endowed guy,' 'the athlete,' 'the dancer'—we were no longer black, we were simply ourselves. The kids in the crew could've been the children of immigrants or ambassadors, Italians or foreigners, living on the periphery or in residential neighborhoods, but the thing that bonded us was a love of hip-hop, which is our universal language."

Ghiorghis got excited while speaking about Piazzale Flaminio. His eyes seemed to light up even more, and from a distance, all his friends watched him making large gestures with his hands. "It was a beautiful experience, but the piazza wasn't enough to make us feel at home. Rome felt constricting, and many of us wanted to leave for one of those places where the people are more mixed. Some left for England, to London; others chose spots even further away and, in the end, the time to leave came for me too."

Hearing him mention London, I was reminded that my departure was nearing, so I asked him how long he'd lived there and what it was like.

In the beginning, it was great and exciting, but with time he realized that outside Italy, it was even harder to respond to the inevitable question. He didn't have the right words to tell his story, and so even abroad, he ended up meeting up with the people who'd been his friends in Piazzale Flaminio. When they were together, they spoke of the past with nostalgia.

"After seven years," he said to me, "I swung by Rome—I had to deal with some things. It was because I'd gotten Italian citizenship. I can't tell you all the trouble I went through—I'd received the draft card and, apparently, since I hadn't shown up, was committing a crime. So many headaches, but when I walked out of the airport, it only took me a second to realize that I had come home, bathed in the light of this city."

"What's the difference between swinging by and returning?"

Ghiorghis responded without hesitation: "For seven years, I hadn't been back—seven years is an eternity, but a cappuccino was all it took to find love again, stronger than ever, not because Rome is how it is, but because with the first cappuccino at a café I found myself."

While saying these things, Ghiorghis got almost emotional, meanwhile I wondered what it really meant to be nostalgic.

Nostalgia is when you miss something, but if you've never actually had it, can you still feel nostalgic? Perhaps nostalgia comes when that thing is something others have and you don't.

Ghiorghis came back to Italy, and his crew is still the same—though when before they'd hang out in Piazzale Flaminio, now they no longer have a set meeting place. But they're always together, and they all have hands that are black like mine.

11

"TO PUT IT simply," the doctor says, "suppose the eye is made up of multiple layers. The impact threw them into disorder, and now we need to see how they'll come back together. Is that clear?"

"What are the chances that . . ."

Doctor Bandanna lets out a sigh and stretches back on his chair, firmly gripping both armrests. Thankfully, his colleague with the necktie isn't here today.

"For you doctors, it doesn't make any difference, does it? If someone starts seeing again or remains blind in one eye, it's all the same to you. In the end, it's not like it's your loss."

"Yabar," he responds (he's learned my name), "in this job, you get used to everything. There are people who lose an eye simply because they bump into some corner, and others to whom much more serious accidents happen and they walk away with only a scratch. We're vulnerable, you'll realize this more and more as you age."

"But do you care, I mean, are you happy when a patient recovers?"

"Of course I am. But it doesn't depend on me alone, you understand?"

"Then who does it depend on?"

"On you, above all. The mind has great healing power. Give it time. Your mother couldn't come today?"

I'm close to telling him that Zia Rosa isn't my mom, but I don't.

"She's coming later," I respond. While they push me to my room, I think about Zia Rosa and go back ten years in my thoughts, to the months following our first meeting at the public library.

We were in the living room of her house, she in the armchair framed by two elephant tusks.

"My father was a fascist," she said, as if to justify them. "In those days, Italians enjoyed going hunting."

"We all have our secrets," replied my mom, laughing. "The sins of men don't concern us."

Then Zia Rosa pulled an old photo album off her bookshelf: "Look, these were taken in Mogadishu after independence. There are some photos from the eighties too."

In our house, my mom and I didn't have any keepsakes—no objects, images, newspapers—not a thing. Mama always says that "memory is a burden, and we Somalis carry it all inside." But she doesn't want to have reminders in front of her every day. That's why our house is so bare, Mama doesn't keep anything. If something isn't used for over two months, she says she needs to "tidy up" and gets rid of it. The same treatment is reserved even for books. "There are libraries," she asserts, and after reading them, she donates them to the bookstalls.

But that day, confronted with the images of her hometown, she was like a child again.

"Come look, Yabar!" she shouted, clapping her hands with enthusiasm. While flipping through the photos, she showed me the Azan bakery—where they sent her to buy bread when she was little, the Croce del Sud restaurant—famous for its cream beignets, the Missione movie theater—which showed spaghetti westerns.

"Oh! Hotel Guleed! Do you remember how, when you were a little boy, we'd go there on Fridays, we'd swim and then eat lunch by the pool? I always ordered the veal scaloppina with lemon—you liked it a lot too—I'd cut it up into teeny, tiny pieces." I racked my brain, but it didn't do any good. Then, suddenly, a memory surfaced: it's my father, he's swimming freestyle in the pool without stopping. I see him from behind, his hands cleaving the water without making a sound, a fast and foamless wake—only an instant, then the image vanishes.

"And now, Aunt Zahra?" Sissi asked her. "Now what's it like?"

"Now Mogadishu is all destroyed, honey," Mama replied with a hint of sadness in her voice.

"But Grandma's grave is there! So that means we'll never be able to go visit her!" my little sister exclaimed.

Zia Rosa told us about how every so often they would put flowers on her grandpa's gravestone and that she'd had to explain to Sissi why her grandma wasn't there too.

"I'll teach you the words to say," Mama then promised, "so that when she appears in your dreams, you can have a nice conversation. Do you know what they say in Somalia? That when a person sleeps, their soul goes to a timeless place where it meets the people who are no longer around and those who are yet to be born. That's why it's important to wake a sleeping person gently, because their soul might need more time to return."

And so from that day forward she began speaking not only to me but also to Sissi almost exclusively in Somali, and in such a natural way that we didn't even realize it. Zia Rosa was so happy about it that she finally found the courage to speak in her mother tongue: contrary to her fears, as a matter of fact, she hadn't completely forgotten it. Who knows if memories have a language? Maybe languages are simply colors that mark off different areas of memory.

Zia Rosa shows up at lunchtime. She went to work early today. It's not as hot out, it rained last night.

"Zia," I ask her, "do you remember those elephant tusks you had in your living room?"

"How do these things pop into your head?"

"I don't know. I was thinking about when you said your father was fascist."

"It's the truth. Anyway, I sold the tusks to a secondhand dealer. But what does it matter now?"

"I mean, are you sure that he was even ideologically? He wasn't just, as they say, 'a man of his time'?"

"There's such a thing as free will, Yabar, the ability to choose. Or do you think human beings are all simply sheep?"

"That's not what I was saying. But, well, the fact that he was married to a Somali woman seems contradictory to me."

"Then go and look up just how many children were born from mixed marriages in those years. Hundreds. My father despised Somalis. My mother's illness and death did nothing but confirm his prejudices. To me, instead, they left only a profound sense of shame. It was as though I'd betrayed my mother. I didn't know how to reconnect with her, I lacked the tools."

"But you could've become like your father. Had his same mentality, I mean."

"I already told you: responsibility is individual. It's what guides our actions. It helps us distinguish what's right from what isn't. And then you two came along. Your mom taught me not to be ashamed of myself and my story. I wouldn't have been born if the Italians hadn't settled in Somalia, you and Zahra most likely wouldn't have come here to Rome, and we would've never met."

"The problem, though, is that Mama, unlike you, decided to get rid of her past, but she never asked for anyone's permission to do so."

"You know very well that's not the case."

While Ghiorghis spoke, raising and lowering his hands, one of his friends came up to us. He was very black, his body long and skinny, his face narrow, and a little triangular beard sprouted from his chin.

"So, little brother, all good?" he asked and, winking at his buddy, stuck out his hand to introduce himself: "Nice to meet you. I'm Libbaan."

The whole "little brother" thing was turning into the catchphrase of the night, and it irritated me that they were all laughing about it behind my back, so to get even I told him: "Do you even know how to say your own name? It's pronounced Libaan, with only one *b*."

The guy suddenly grew serious and asked: "How do you know that?" Meanwhile Ghiorghis watched me very closely. I still hadn't revealed where I was from, but now the language had spoken for me.

The boy who doubled the *b* in his name told me I was very lucky because he didn't speak any Somali, not even a word. "No one ever told me how to pronounce my name, or if they did, I've forgotten."

"My mom speaks and sings in Somali all the time," I replied, "but I have problems with it too—I think I understand everything, but I can't speak it."

I'd warmed up a bit, and then, I don't know how, between one thing and the next, I began telling them about the time some Somali women came to see us, many years ago, when I was in first grade. Mama had them sit in the living room. She came back with a thermos of cardamom tea and a blue tin of Danish cookies. They spoke, seated on the couch, while I played silently nearby, because at the time I was still a calm child and didn't seek out adult attention. I even remember that there was some music on in the background. Many weeks had passed since we'd heard from my father; he'd spent long periods away before but had always kept in touch with us. Mama had dark circles under her eyes and was trying to hide her worries from me.

She abruptly stood up and went to the stereo to turn up the volume. The women asked: "Why are you turning up the music if your son doesn't understand Somali?"

And she replied: "He understands, he understands everything."

They began speaking intensely. Part of me could barely follow along, part of me didn't find what they were saying very interesting. Until one of them raised her voice at my mom: "We told you not to trust your husband—those wild dogs raided our homes, killed our men, and they still aren't satisfied."

Hearing these words, my mom yelled at the women to leave and never to speak like that in front of me again. She told them several times that my father would never kill anyone. The women looked at her, taken aback, and told her to calm down. But my mom couldn't calm herself and, after showing them out, she shut herself in the bathroom. I pulled on the door handle so she'd open the door and asked her over and over: "Who are the wild dogs? Who killed? Where's Papa, Aabbe?"

Since that day, my mom made a habit of turning up the volume of the music when she spoke on the phone or someone came to see her—she was afraid of what I might hear. Naturally, this only increased my curiosity, and that's how I discovered Mama was desperately trying to convince my father to come back and that she feared for his life. Unfortunately—but I only understood this later—Aabbe was too tangled up in the war to come back and live with us.

While I was saying all these things out loud that sounded strange even to my ears, I realized it was the first time I'd spoken so openly about certain family matters, and I'd only just met these people. Who knows what had gotten into me.

Libaan, moved by the story he'd just heard, began telling me his own. He also, at first, lived in Somalia with both his parents. He was ten when the war broke out, and his parents decided to seek refuge in Italy. Unfortunately, they were not able to obtain a visa for his mother, so he and his father left without her, in the hope of sending her documents and a ticket at a later date. Months passed, his father was buried in bureaucratic hassles, there was never enough money and, at a certain point, he decided to put Libaan in boarding school, promising he'd be back for him soon. But things went differently than planned. After some time, he forgot about both his wife and his son, who he never went back to find. As he grew up, Libaan, in turn, forgot everything he knew—even how to pronounce his own name—because there was no longer anyone to correct him. He learned Italian, and the new words canceled out the old. His mother's voice, though, he'd never forgotten.

My father, too, for all I knew, had forgotten about me and my mother, but at least the two of us were still together.

When he was eighteen, Libaan had also become part of the Flaminio crew, and having finished high school, he left the boarding school and set about searching for his mom. He went to the Somali consulate to ask for information, but no one listened to him. Libaan knew the names of his mother and the village where she lived, but they explained to him that the name of the person was not needed, not even that of the place in which they lived—if he wanted to find his mother, he had to know the name of the clan she belonged to. Libaan didn't remember it, or maybe he'd never known it.

Twenty years had passed since the last time he'd seen his mother when, out of the blue, his father showed up. It couldn't be a coincidence. Libaan insisted so much that the man finally got him his mother's number. Libaan was so excited he ran to call her straight away. But his mom didn't speak his new language, and Libaan no longer understood the old. At one point, someone tore the phone from her hand—an uncle, a relative—and in the confusion, Libaan only recognized one message that they kept repeating to him in Italian: "Money, money, to you mother send money," as if after so many years the only thing she wanted from her son was money. But he himself didn't even have enough to live on. He hung up, upset, but still remembered the phone number.

When the story was over, we were so shaken up that no one said anything for a few minutes, until Ghiorghis, jumping up from the moped, had an idea. "Listen, little brother, I really don't think we met by chance. I mean, your friends ditched you, you stayed outside, and there just has to be a reason that we're here together tonight, talking."

The story had moved me so much that I no longer felt like provoking. Then again, I couldn't repress a vision—Zia Rosa's face attached to Ghiorghis's body. How come certain people think that ordinary incidents hold some deeper meaning? His idea was that we could all go together to a nearby call center and ring Libaan's mother. I tried to explain to him that I'd only pronounced a name correctly and didn't feel up to speaking in Somali on the telephone.

The two of them soon were in league. Ghiorghis was the pushier one: "You said you have to go to London, no? This way you'll start practicing—what language do you think you'll be speaking there? Come on, it doesn't cost you anything!"

"But it's late, at this hour they'll all be asleep. It's about two a.m. in Somalia."

"Even better. This way we can be sure they're home."

They were so insistent that, in the end, I had to give in: "All right, I'll try."

It was almost midnight when I went with Libaan to call, and even though it was far from hot out, we were both sweating heavily. I was sweating because I felt like I no longer remembered a word of Somali, he because he'd be speaking to his mother for the first time in twenty years.

The call center was a cramped little store with many glass booths inside. There were signs in various languages, and through the transparent walls you could see people talking—each of them moved their mouths in a different way, but you couldn't hear their voices; they were like fish packed inside an aquarium.

As soon as we walked in, the manager, a man with a white beard, asked us: "Where do you want to call?" And we explained the situation to him so that he'd give us a phone with two receivers, since Libaan and I needed to both talk and listen.

After a few minutes, he lets us into a booth with two handsets—the space is very narrow, and it's hot as hell. We're sweaty, the air is boiling, the phone number endless, the calling code endless, and the time it takes them to pick up endless. I feel like I'm in a damp cave, and I picture the telephone at the other end also in a place like this—a boiling hot cavern like ours with Libaan's mother who's been inside waiting for twenty years. The phone rings, I wait for a voice, and Libaan stares at me because he's afraid of my silence. He tells me, "You got this!" and from the other end I hear: "Halow, yaa waaye?" Hello, who is it? They're speaking in Somali, and I understand everything, but until now I've only ever transformed Somali into Italian—I don't know how to transform Italian into Somali.

From the other end of the line, they repeat, "Halow?" And Libaan says, "You got this!" again, and I see the words line up in my head, I feel and see all of them, they kick and take shape like whole walnuts, and I push with my forehead and my eyes to get them out. The words are hard, they cut through my head like when it's hot out and you drink something icy cold. I feel a stabbing pain between my eyes and catch my breath. But the pain still doesn't stop, so I start pushing again, pushing hard, and now I feel the words come to my throat, and I touch their shape with my tongue. I push air out, and the words spill out whole from my mouth.

I see Libaan smiling at me and saying, "Mama, it's me," his voice cracking, and I repeat, voice cracking, the same words, "Hooyo, waa aniga," and the words "Mama," "it's," and "me" sound the same in the new language, maybe just a bit drier. Libaan is frantic, and he wants to talk about too many things at once: about how much he searched for her, how much he's missed her, how much he's thought of her, but he's only able to say simple words and his mother says the same things, and I'm the mother and the son at the same time.

We're in the cave, and the air is boiling. Libaan and I are both all sweaty, and we're each holding a handset attached to one cord.

The voice of his mother reaches both of us, and our voices reach her together. I feel the words whole in my mouth, it'd been a long time since I'd felt them, and these words are the words of the son and they're also mine—Libaan and I together say, "Hooyo," Mama, and "waa aniga," it's me.

12

WHEN I WAS a boy, I spent a brief period at the Città dei Ragazzi, the same boarding school that Libaan and Ghiorghis grew up in, but they were older than me and we never crossed paths. It's located at the end of Via della Pisana, outside Rome, a little walled city surrounded by olive trees and vineyards. The pedagogical principle guiding the teachers is self-government—they maintain that only by learning to take responsibility will students adjust well and not become criminals. The kids in the "city" even meet in assembly to elect their own mayor, who in turn nominates the council members to help them oversee life in the city. There are other posts, various roles that can be appointed—the banker, the restaurant owner, the judge—but at the time I was too young to perform any of them. We all had to do the cleaning, wait tables, help in the kitchen, and perform other simple tasks. A domestic currency circulated in the Città dei Ragazzi called the shield, which you'd earn by participating in activities and then could spend however you liked.

I've never spoken to Sissi or the Sybarite about the experience, maybe because it didn't last long, and anyway it was so traumatic that I preferred to repress it. But for Ghiorghis it'd been different.

His mother was working as a maid for a rich Roman family, she lived with them and went to fetch him on the weekends. With time, the family grew fond of him too, and his mother got permission to bring her son to live with them. Ghiorghis, however, chose to stay in the "city" with all his friends.

My mom never would've wanted to send me to boarding school, but she was obligated to—she no longer trusted anyone, she had to change her life—but at the time these were things I couldn't understand.

She told me, "It's a nice place, you just have to hang in there for a few months," and, unceremoniously, left me with one of the chaperones. I remember the girl, looking down at me with an obnoxious smile, telling Mama not to worry, that she had made the right choice and shouldn't feel hurt if when she came to visit I didn't pay much attention to her, because that's what the kids always do. She spoke as though I wasn't there listening to her, as though I were deaf or dumb. The fact is that even if you're only six years old, you understand a bunch of things, much more than the grown-ups think.

I burst into tears, of course, but Mama remained impassive. Drying my tears with a handkerchief, she said: "Don't embarrass me, adkayso," which essentially means "Keep it together." Maybe she could've said more to me, but it was all very difficult for her too.

She had lost a lot of weight, was hardly sleeping, and had stopped singing, and my father hadn't been around for some time. I would ask her over and over again: "Where's Aabbe?" And all she'd say was that there'd been a tragedy. I didn't understand what tragedy she was referring to. Was Aabbe dead?

"No, worse," she eventually responded, then in a whisper: "There's been a homicide." I didn't know what a homicide was, and Mama didn't want to explain it to me. No wonder she always turned up the volume of the music, she wanted to keep the tragedy hidden. I thought it was all my fault—the tragedy and

Aabbe's absence. One time, I let slip that he'd brought me to a secret place and I wasn't supposed to tell her. It was so nice to ride on his shoulders and drink aranciata, what did I know about the wild dogs who'd killed our men and raided our houses?

"What did your father say? Who were the men there with him?" But I didn't know anyone, I only knew that everyone listened to him as if he were their boss. A stranger had even come to meet them—he was Italian, and to make arrangements, they had to speak in his language. Maybe my father hadn't understood that the commander of the river should use his power for the good of everyone and not for his own interests. In the fable, the giant anthill and the garas tree are only used to scare the crocodiles, not to kill innocent people. Maybe that's why the tragedy had taken place, I told myself.

Anyway, eventually I adapted to boarding school life. It wasn't a bad place—there was the school, the pool, the soccer field; we ate in the cafeteria and slept in big bedrooms. There were many of us but no distinctions were made, the adults indiscriminately distributed food, affection, and lessons to everyone. Still, each of us wished for an adult that was ours alone, an adult who found us special. The longer you stayed, the more you learned to do without parents. We kids became like siblings—the older ones took care of the younger, the younger ones relied on the older. At night, we told stories where our parents turned into a hot-air balloon: we kids stayed on the ground while the hot-air balloon drifted away on its own, up in the sky.

I made a best friend in boarding school, named Amilcare—his parents were from Cape Verde, and they'd chosen his name in honor of an important figure who'd liberated all the people of the archipelago.

We loved doing battle royales. We had some good warriors and some bad, but we never fought against one another—Amilcare and I were always allied together against the bad guys.

One afternoon after doing homework, since it was hot out and a beautiful day, we sat down on the lawn to set up our armies. It took us a long time to meticulously prepare the battlefield, almost more than for the actual battle. We gathered rocks, moss, pine cones, leaves, sticks, and other things we could find in the boarding school's park.

While we were stretched out in the grass playing, I looked up and saw a man in the distance. He looked like my father, but I didn't think it could possibly be him, I thought I was mistaken. He was tall and skinny and wearing a very elegant suit. As he gradually came closer the resemblance grew, but I was still afraid of deluding myself. I stayed motionless with my stomach glued to the lawn, and my eyes sharpened, like a toy soldier in the trenches. My father saw me and smiled, stretching out his arms. His face lit up, and he said: "Won't you come say hello?"

Then, without even responding to Amilcare, who asked me, "Is that man your father?" I jumped up on my skinny little legs and threw my arms around his neck. Papa picked me up and hugged me.

"Now this is truly a happy day!" He said that at least three times while kissing my forehead and repeating "wiilkayga," my boy.

After hugging like that for a while, he said he'd be taking me out for a day in the city. I felt a bit disappointed because I'd hoped he'd come back for good and that he'd be taking me away from boarding school. He took my hand, and we went to the teacher to ask for permission to go out. The woman looked at his identification, filled out a form for my father to sign, and let us go.

The car he'd come to pick me up in was very elegant, there was even a driver. When we sat down, I asked him where he'd been all that time and why Mama had said that "there's been a homicide." I repeated the words I'd learned by heart without understanding what they meant. My father twitched. For a moment, I seemed to see a different light in his eyes—they'd turned almost yellow, like those of crocodiles. But my anxiety vanished as soon as he began talking.

He told me that these things were too complicated for a child, that he had looked for me and hadn't even known I was in boarding school, but thankfully his informants had found me. I asked him what informants were, and he only said that Mama had hidden me and she didn't want us to see each other, but I had to stay calm because I was his son and he would take care of everything. As for "Omicidio," it was just a nickname they'd given him for his courage, in fact, he was famous for having fought a crocodile barehanded.

I decided that my father was a hero and that he was right—it truly was a happy day. He brought me to the carnival rides, we went to buy some new clothes for me and, so we'd always remember how happy we'd been, we slipped into one of those booths where people take their passport photos. We selected the option that took four different photos, so each time we could hug each other in a different way, all while trying to fit our faces in the frame. In the end, he brought me to a restaurant, but it was still early, the tables were all empty. We sat across from each other, and I began feeling sad because the day was ending. But Papa said we had to put on a brave face and enjoy our dinner.

We ordered a cotoletta and french fries for me, spinach and roast chicken for him, plus a bottle of Coca-Cola in my honor. My father, with his large appetite, picked the chicken clean and, once he'd finished, told me he was going to the bathroom to wash his hands. After a few minutes, I felt a pang in my chest, as though my father had left without me again, and I ran to the bathroom to look for him. It was a room for men only, there were many sinks and a long mirror on the wall in front of a row of urinals. I didn't see him at first because he was in a corner, and he didn't notice me either. It was just the two of us in there. My father had his back to me, he was washing something that he held in his fingers, and the mirror reflected his forehead and eyes.

Seeing my reflection behind his, he seemed almost surprised, and he whipped around. That was when I saw his bare gums—in his fingers, he was holding dentures with four upper incisors. His gums were purple and his eyes yellow, like those of crocodiles.

I screamed, scared to death—back then, I didn't know that younger men can have fake teeth too—and my father looked surprised, as if he hadn't just eaten at the same table with me, as if the teacher hadn't looked at his identification and said, "All right, you can go," as if he hadn't taken my hand and brought me to the rides. I had never been afraid of my father before that moment, and that was the last time I saw him.

The commander of the river is the best swimmer in Somalia, they say he's the only one capable of swimming alongside the crocodiles. He knows all the secrets to control them—he knows how to bewitch them with medicinal plants when he calls them out of the water and how to persuade them to obey his orders.

The crocodiles are part of the river, and the commander has an important role, which is why men and women bring him animals, fruit, and bread. If someone refuses to pay him tribute, the commander calls to a crocodile and orders it to stretch out on top of the person, and in a blink of the eye they disappear under the animal.

Men and women can only live in the village so long as they pay their tributes, and they can also ask the commander for concessions. If, for example, a woman is in debt to a man and she refuses to pay him, the man can go to the commander and tell him about it. If he has brought fruit, meat, and grains, the commander will call nine crocodiles to capture the woman while she's at the river fetching water. They'll capture her, and one of the crocodiles will carry the woman on its back, two will keep guard on the right and two on the left, two will swim ahead, two behind, and they'll bring her before the commander. The woman will have no alternative but to pay the debt that she hadn't wanted to settle. The commander will feed the crocodiles for their help, and they'll silently return to the river to wait for a new assignment.

"The wise men appoint the commander to govern over the lives of the crocodiles and the people, but in the story, the commander uses the crocodiles and uses the people—are using and governing the same thing?"

My mother smiles and says: "Good observation. The commander of the river was elected by the people, so you'd assume that he would act in everyone's interest. Still, we can't be certain that the commander knows how to distinguish the people from the crocodiles or his own interests from those of the people. Do you think you would be able to?"

Some rivers, when they flood, make the surrounding land fertile. The water overflows, and the nutrients spill out. They say fantastic treasures, precious pearls, mercenary lances, Garibaldian pistols, white marble statues, and ancient candelabras are safeguarded on the bed of the Tiber. Naturally, there are also other things at the bottom of the river—carcasses, wrecks, carrion—and when they surface they must be cleared away because they can accumulate under the bridges and block the flow. One time, under Ponte Sisto, some sort of huge dam formed, made up of logs and branches dragged by the current. Civil Defense had to remove it, but I had so enjoyed watching that dead forest hugging the white bastions.

When the water reaches the alert level, seagulls sit on the water as though to imitate the ducks, and only by observing them can you understand just how fast the river is moving. The seagulls glide on the surface, they let themselves be carried, they don't resist and don't sink like the swallow I'd wanted to save.

I, too, wanted to be like a seagull that night. After having exchanged phone numbers with Ghiorghis and Libaan, I walked home. I needed to calm down, plus I'd always hated buses, especially the night ones. I tried to remember what my father's face looked like, but I couldn't picture anything more than a black oval with no features. Mama had made all his photographs disappear, but I found some in my secret box, the one where as a boy I'd kept coins from around the world, shells, postcards, and other little things.

My secret box looks like a miniature piece of furniture: it's made of floral-printed cardboard and has three little drawers. In one I'd kept the four passport photos my father and I had taken together when I was in boarding school. In the pictures you could see two faces always partially cut off, a man and a boy having fun coming in and out of the frame.

I'd forgotten what he looked like, and now I saw him smiling in the shadows, as though we were playing hide-and-seek. Our faces were never complete, so I grabbed some scissors to separate his face from mine and a poster board to attach the various pieces to. I'd gotten it into my head that I had to put our faces back together in order to see him again, but the pieces didn't fit together and so the result was monstrous—one eye bigger than the other, his mouth on his neck, his forehead too low.

I no longer remembered what he looked like, and now this was the only image I had left of him.

I ask the nurse permission to go down to the café with the Sybarite. It takes a bit of begging, but in the end she consents, so long as I'm not gone for too long. I buy my usual newspaper, furtively scan the local news pages, then we order two cans of cold peach tea at the counter and head off toward the courtyard porticoes. There's a white marble fountain in the center where a dolphin spits water into a shell and in the recesses they've put cyclamens and ferns. There are two basins, one inside the other, and all around there are small blue steps. On the rocks a dozen water turtles are sunbathing, and others are swimming among the algae. I get a little closer.

"What are you doing?" asks my friend.

"I wonder if after all these years I'd still be able to recognize him."

He stares at me, taken aback.

"Do you remember that little turtle I had when I was younger? Back when I still went with Mama to work, right after we moved, we often walked past a pet store. I always wanted to go in, but Mama would have none of it. Do you know what she'd nicknamed the store owner? 'The Animal Torturer!' 'Go ahead, go say hello to the Animal Torturer,' she'd whisper, pushing me toward the entrance. In the end, after much insistence, I convinced her to buy me a little water turtle. She agreed on the condition that I would be the one to take care of it."

"Now I remember. It was in a colored tank with an island and a small palm tree. It had a strange name, right?"

"His name was Amilcare."

The turtles are various sizes, but they all look so much alike that it's impossible to distinguish one from another.

"Only you could give a name like that to a turtle!"

"It was the name of my best friend in boarding school."

"Boarding school? You went to a boarding school?"

"Yeah."

"How come you never told me about it?"

"Dunno, it never came up."

"Are you still in touch after all these years? Have you ever seen this Amilcare guy again?"

"No, never."

"And what happened to the turtle?"

"Mama complained because between his poop and his feed, he made the whole house stink, also because I never remembered to change the water. One day, she happened to be here at the hospital, for an appointment I think, and she saw this big basin. It probably wasn't allowed, but she decided to get rid of him and persuaded me that Amilcare would be much happier here, together with all the other little turtles. She also said we'd come visit him every so often."

"Did you ever come visit?"

"Of course not. You know what my mama's like. She has bigger things to worry about."

"Sorry, but why did she send you to boarding school? Didn't she have anyone to leave you with?" The Sybarite has a hard time believing that there's a period of my life he knows nothing about.

"That's what I've always wondered myself. The truth, in my opinion, is that when it came to her family, she felt indebted and maybe also guilty. Do you remember the day we went with her to send some money?"

My friend laughs, throwing his head back.

Not even a year has passed since Mama came to pick us up at Termini, having returned from a school trip. We'd been in Calabria. Sissi had picked a bunch of yellow daisies and, because she found them extraordinarily beautiful, had put them in a plastic cup full of water so they wouldn't wilt.

"For our mothers!" she'd said, even though Zia Rosa was the only one who truly appreciated fresh flowers. Mama, however, had hugged her with gratitude and stuck the plastic cup between the front seats of the car.

"I have to stop by the Money Transfer for a moment," she said. "It'll only take a second—you guys can come in if you want, or wait for me in the car. Up to you."

"Who do you have to send money to this time?" I asked her, irritated, while Sissi shot me a dirty look. She knew we always argued about this.

Mama got out of the car, fuming, and dismissed me with her usual line: "You really never give up, do you?"

The request for money always came from above. It was often an elder of the family who called, interceding on behalf of a relative who needed help. "But can't she just refuse to send money to whoever is requesting it?" the Sybarite asked as soon as Mama had gotten out.

"Never mind," Sissi intervened. "Don't you start too."

"I'm just trying to understand," he defended himself. "It doesn't seem to me like you're swimming in money."

"Yes, but she saves up, she puts money aside. She says to refuse would be a terrible offense."

"Even if she's never met the relative? Even if you've been living far away from everyone for a thousand years?"

"Auntie explained it to us," Sissi added. "It's a cultural issue," as if "cultural issues" were fossils from the Stone Age.

"Sorry, but what does that have to do with anything? What about us? Who's helped us?"

"Auntie says that if you need help, all you have to do is ask."

"Yes, too bad the only person she has that close a relationship with is your mom. Does that seem logical to you?" I turned to the Sybarite.

"I don't know. Well, considering that it's just the two of you, I guess not. Just think, it was my grandparents who bought my parents' house for them. But they, at most, feel responsible for us kids, nothing more. The elders who call and ask you to send money for the family . . . seems like the Mafia!"

"But it's only right, a redistribution of wealth!"

"Just shut up!" I responded to Sissi. This is what she does to make me mad.

"I'd get it if she were sending money to her parents, to immediate relatives. Every so often, in fact, she tries to shut me up by saying, 'Wait, so you wouldn't help me if I were struggling?' As if it didn't mean anything that she's the one who brought me into the world, fed, clothed, and raised me, and all on her own, no less."

Mama, in the meantime, had gotten back in the car and, while starting it, made sure that the unstable little vase of flowers wouldn't spill.

"I, for example"—I turned to her as though she'd participated in our conversation—"if Sissi and the Sybarite were struggling, would send them all the money in the world." At which my friends huddled around me, playfully poking and pulling at me.

13

AFTER THE EVENING spent with Ghiorghis and Libaan outside Cantiere, I didn't leave the house. The phone kept ringing, and I knew it was the Sybarite, but I had no desire to pick up. He even came to lean on the buzzer a couple of times. Being mad at Sissi and the Sybarite helped me feel calmer about leaving for London. After all, what did my friends know about the war, about the past?

I would spend the entire day on the couch in front of the television, and when my mom got home, I'd go out just long enough for a beer. Seeing me come back in after not even an hour, she'd start grumbling: "I sure am glad you're leaving! I'm sick and tired of having you around!" But every time I asked her questions about London, about why she was sending me there, she simply responded that that was her decision and she'd made it for my sake.

"I can't protect you forever, it's time you learned how to fend for yourself."

The fact is, apart from doing badly in school, I've always obeyed my mother. I would never dream of not doing what she tells me to.

"Waryaa, I'm not another one of your friends!" she warns me the rare times I try to state my case. According to my mother, our relationship is based on a single irrefutable principle: the absolute recognition of her authority.

Anyway, while I was sitting in my usual catatonic state in front of the screen, a story on the news caught my attention. They were talking about a suicide bomber who'd attempted to set off a bomb in the London metro. He'd made it himself using a hair product with hydrogen peroxide and whole-wheat flour specifically for roti, a round bread that Indians make. Thankfully, the concoction didn't come out right, and in the end, all the bomb did was make a lot of noise, like a huge corn kernel popping. I can almost see him, the bomber, loading up on bottles in an African beauty supply store, then playing little chemist with the wrong formula!

After the explosion, the bomber had escaped by jumping out of a train window, and he'd changed his clothes in the public restrooms. Didn't he know there are cameras all over the metro stations? The images showed this calm-looking guy in a white undershirt, trying to blend in with all the people.

After a few days of searching internationally they'd caught him right here in Rome—of all the places he could've been—hidden in a relative's house. The bomber had gotten himself some fake papers, and he'd run to his poor brother, who'd been living in Italy for years and had a normal job. They said on the news that he'd been caught at night and showed the house, a nondescript apartment building in the suburbs. His brother was put in prison too, even though he had nothing to do with it, because by hiding him, he'd become an accomplice. I started buying the newspaper every day because of the bomber. The whole saga had made so much of an impression on me that I wanted to follow all of its developments.

His lawyer argued that he hadn't intended to kill anyone, but just to draw attention. He was infuriated about all the women and children dying in Iraq at the hands of Americans, and he wanted, with the bomb, to express his protest. We all have moments when we're mad at the world, but to decide to blow yourself up in the middle of a bunch of people is an entirely different thing, I'd say.

Nonetheless, at the thought of the bomber shouting out, "Allahu Akbar," while the bomb misfires in his hands with a cloud of foam I, to be honest, almost peed myself laughing. I still wouldn't have wanted to be there in front of him, of course. The newspapers all said more or less the same things, and they showed the photo of him in a white undershirt along with the one of the Roman apartment where they'd caught him. At least until, unexpectedly, an article came out that nearly gave me a heart attack. The journalist had tracked down one of the bomber's ex-girlfriends and had interviewed her. The two of them, when they were about my age, had been part of the Flaminio crew. The bomber was nicknamed "Bambi" because of his big, black, fawn-like eyes and his thick lashes. The girl had been so shocked to see his face on TV. According to her, besides being handsome, he was also extremely kind, which is why he had so much success with the ladies. They used to go to the discoteca on Saturday afternoons, and like everybody else, Bambi loved hip-hop—he was a great dancer and dressed like a rappettaro, with sagging pants and jerseys from various basketball teams. His idols were African American rappers from the ghetto, but he wasn't a violent guy. He kept his distance from the wrong crowd; if there were fights, which there often were, he was always the peacemaker.

You could find good people in Piazzale Flaminio, like the two of them, but also dangerous people—pushers and petty thieves. That's why the police would often go there for a raid. Who knows how many times they must've asked him for his papers too?

He was Muslim but didn't have any issues hanging out with people who weren't. He didn't eat pork, of course, but didn't consider alcohol a taboo. The times they had talked about faith, he said he believed in Allah, that's it—he wasn't an extremist. He had left for London, like many other kids from the Horn of Africa, to get political asylum. Mainly, he'd wanted to be in a place where there was more going on—all he cared about was having fun—and more job opportunity. In Rome, he hadn't been able to do anything very serious: he worked from time to time, but he didn't have any real goals, and they didn't trust him; that's why he couldn't make plans for the future.

Up until that moment, no newscast had said the bomber had grown up in Rome, so you can imagine my reaction when I found out he used to hang around Piazzale Flaminio too. I called Ghiorghis right away to see if he knew him. Ghiorghis didn't seem surprised to hear from me: "Where've you been, little brother?"

"Nowhere, I've had a ton of stuff to do. I'm leaving soon, remember?" I replied from my spot sprawled out on the couch. I told him that the story about the bomber had shaken me. When I asked if he'd known him and said how I thought he might have because they must've been around the same age, Ghiorghis told me that if I wanted to talk about it, we had to meet in person, because it was dangerous over the phone. He added that the people in his old crew would have much to say on the subject too. His concerns and tone seemed a bit exaggerated to me but, given how little I knew him, he came across as someone who smelled conspiracy everywhere—Ghiorghis is the type that lets himself be influenced by the movies and thinks those sorts of things happen in real life.

We agreed to meet at Termini. He would come pick me up with his moped, and then we'd go to Ex Snia, an occupied centro sociale where his friends would be.

Ghiorghis drove with his helmet unfastened, and because he tilted his head to the right to talk to me, I worried that we'd suddenly find ourselves on the sidewalk and would crash into a wall. But in the end, I have no idea how, he managed to keep us headed in the right direction.

He, too, was surprised that no newspaper had reported the news. "Bambi didn't grow up in Africa or London as they'd like to have people believe, but in Rome, just like us."

"What difference does it make? Why don't they just say it?" I asked while we passed Piazza Vittorio.

"To avoid responsibility—they don't want anything to do with us, much less if we're wanted as criminals."

"What do you mean? We who?"

"Those of us who grew up here, children of Eritrean, Ethiopian, Somali parents—from the ex-colonies, in other words. The Italians don't even know we exist. Do you know how my mother ended up in Rome?"

"No."

"She was working as a maid for a Magneti Marelli executive down in Ethiopia. The guy had been there with his entire family for generations, I think. When Mengistu seized power, he kicked all the Italians out, so my mom accepted her employers' offer and followed them to Italy."

"Had you already been born?"

"No, I was born here in Rome. She sent me to Africa for the first few years and my grandma raised me, then when I was old enough she brought me back to Italy and sent me to boarding school."

Ghiorghis's phone started ringing. I hoped he wouldn't pick up given his already dangerous driving, but he went ahead and stuck it between his helmet and ear.

"Hey, I'm on my way."

"Careful! We'll crash!" I yelled at him, at which he cut the call short with: "If I don't hang up this kid will lose his shit!"

Then, because I was dying of curiosity, I asked him: "So? Did you know Bambi or not?"

"Of course, we were in boarding school together."

"In your opinion, why'd he do it? The bomb, I mean."

"Dunno, probably because of religion, what can I say? You're Muslim too, right?"

"I'm circumcised and everything, and I've even tried to be religious, but I didn't succeed."

"Succeed?" Ghiorghis laughed. "Why, religion is something you have to be successful at?"

"Well, yes, in the sense that even I would like to have a principle, a faith, something to believe in. The fact is that I'm not successful even when I make an effort. But on the other hand, if the risk is becoming like the bomber, at this point it's better to stay a heathen."

"You know what? The truth is he was a wimp. When he was little, he always said he missed his mommy, so the teachers treated him with more care. He got more attention and the best gifts—the latest stereo, the fastest skates, the coolest sweatshirt—also because he was handsome, that smartass."

I thought about how bitter Ghiorghis was that Bambi got the best gifts, and I wanted to tease him about being jealous, but I couldn't come up with a good line.

"Do you think he wanted to blow himself up and kill a ton of people or just stir up some trouble?"

"Both," he replied. "If you think about it, deep down it's the same principle: a search for attention."

"Yes, but if the attempt succeeds, you die and you kill a bunch of people along with you. How can someone even remotely think that's the right thing to do?"

We'd gone a good distance down Via Prenestina in the meantime, and since our destination was on the left-hand side of the road, Ghiorghis did a big U-turn. I wasn't expecting it and nearly slid off the back of the moped.

Ex Snia is an abandoned factory where they used to make rayon; it had been occupied and transformed into a centro sociale a dozen years ago.

"They made parachutes here," said Ghiorghis.

"Parachutes?"

"Yes, and tents, uniforms, and backpacks for soldiers during the war."

There's a big park surrounding Snia, unfortunately mostly off-limits.

Basically, as Ghiorghis told me, a famous developer had wanted to build a shopping mall there and who knows what else but, while digging, the workers struck an aquifer with extremely pure water. "For a while, the guy played dumb, he was afraid they'd revoke his permit. He had the water drawn out with pumps and emptied in the sewer. Until a storm made a mess of the whole thing, and that's how the lake came to be."

While talking, we'd gone deep enough in the pine grove to be able to admire the lake through a metal fence.

"That's an incredible story," I tell him. "But why is it closed off?"

"Well, the developer still won't give up, the neighborhood and the centro sociale kids have been fighting for years for this to become a public park. Come on, let's turn back. You see that small building? That's where we're headed. I want you to meet some people."

His Flaminio friends were all outside under a row of small trees. Libaan, seeing me coming, ran up and hugged me. They were talking about other things, but an impatient Ghiorghis blurted out that they had to tell me about Bambi. This made everyone, including me, feel embarrassed. Then, because it bothered me how he'd put me on the spot, I told him: "Would you quit using me to get attention?" But my remark rolled off his back, or maybe he just didn't let his reaction show. Instead, it served to break the ice. One by one they all began to talk.

The first was Libaan. He spoke about one of their friends who had just gotten out of prison, a guy who had a major alcohol problem and kept getting into trouble, for which, every now and again, they would lock him up. Anyway, they had met recently for a coffee but ended up ordering beer instead, and the friend told him that the night they'd caught Bambi, all the Ethiopians, Eritreans, and Somalis in the prison had been awakened. They'd lined them all up, then had shown the bomber to each of them. Everyone had denied knowing him, and this friend did the same. He'd lied, of course, but then again, Bambi had changed so much that he had struggled to recognize him.

Someone from the group interrupted to say that he had seen Bambi a couple times when he'd come to Rome on vacation, and Bambi had seemed fine to him. Someone else had seen him in London some years before, and already at that point he had seemed different. He was dating a Christian Ethiopian who he'd forced to convert and convinced to wear the headscarf.

I, too, thought that religion didn't have anything to do with it. I had gotten angry many times, but had never started making bombs in the name of Allah.

For example, one day I was on the bus and I had to get off at the next stop. I was up near the driver, so I asked him: "Would you open the door for me, please?"

And the guy said: "How many times do I have to tell you people to exit through the rear door?"

I looked around and, since there was no one else nearby, I said, "Why use the plural if I'm the only one here? Why say 'tell you people'? Who do you have to tell?" The driver got even angrier and refused to open the door. After a few long seconds, he got up and stood right in front of me. I was a head taller than him, but he thought he was a big deal. He was one of those guys who pumps iron.

I lost my cool and insulted him: "Fuckin' beefcake!"

And he yelled back: "Go home, beat it!" pointing toward the rear doors.

Then the people on the bus started grumbling, "Just get off the damn bus!"

They were talking to me and not the driver, who I'd simply asked to open the door in front. While getting off through the back, I honestly thought that I would happily plant a bomb on that bus so they'd all be blown up—the driver and the people yelling at me.

Maybe the bomber had thought: I'd happily plant a bomb somewhere. And then he'd literally gone and done it. We say lots of things that we then don't do and that we'd never do: I don't know if Bambi actually wanted to set off the bomb and kill a lot of people. Maybe it's true that he just wanted to attract attention, so he mixed up the ingredients badly on purpose.

While I was all caught up in my thoughts, one of Ghiorghis's friends—a tiny guy, short and with a very light skin tone, so light he looked Arab—began talking. He was furious. He didn't seem much older than the others, but his hair was all white.

Bambi had been his friend for a long time; they'd drank, smoked, and talked together. "Who knows?" he said. "Maybe one day he could've just shown up like old times: 'Let's have a cigarette. Drink a beer,' and *boom*—blown us all up." The guy was twitching a ton, he looked like a marionette: "Yes, he would've blown us all up, *boom*, just because some of us are Christians!"

In response I said, "But you were friends—religion has nothing to do with it. He never would've blown you up."

But the guy only got more agitated: "It's his fault that they're now more racist than ever."

Then, while Ghiorghis looked at me with a baffled expression, I asked, "Who's more racist than ever?"

I began unbuttoning my shirt because of the heat. Seeing the white tank top I was wearing underneath, suddenly everyone stopped talking. After a bit, Ghiorghis shook his head and said: "To tell you the truth, little brother, Bambi even looks like you . . . the two of you really look alike." And he came over to give me a slap on the back. This time, he had gotten the last word.

14

MY DEPARTURE FOR London was closer than ever. Even the Sybarite had made peace with it and had stopped seeking me out. I spent the final days moping around the house. The heat was suffocating, so I kept one of those spray bottles near me, the kind for watering plants that my mom used for ironing.

I felt strange after all those hours on my own—I don't know, at certain points my heart started pounding harder out of the blue, an absurd and terrifying sensation, almost like I was short of breath. Good thing I'd accepted an invite from Ghiorghis and Libaan; they wanted to have a barbecue in my honor before I left. I loved the idea both because I adore grilled meat and because I couldn't believe they had the guts to barbecue in the middle of Villa Borghese.

They told me it wouldn't be the first time they met up there. Their last barbecue had been planned for the anniversary of the fascists' March on Rome, no less, the same day in which, years ago, the Piazzale Flaminio station had been inaugurated. A real slap in the face—if they'd had the guts to do one then, why wouldn't they now?

So we made a plan: they'd find me in the piazzale, I would help them unload and—most importantly—help them light the grill.

It's something I've always liked doing; my mom taught me an infallible method with a tin can. You take an empty tomato puree can, remove the top and bottom, and set it on the charcoal. Inside the can go a couple Diavolina lighter cubes along with some small pieces of charcoal, then you toss in a lit match or piece of paper—it works 100 percent of the time. I'm also good at stoking the fire. If you don't have a straw fan, you can use sheets of paper, newspapers, or magazines, and vigorously fan underneath until the charcoal in the center turns red and incandescent. At that point, you remove the can, freeing the glowing embers, and the charcoal will ignite completely.

While describing the procedure to him in great detail over the phone, Ghiorghis was blatantly skeptical. He thought no one could be better than him at lighting the grill—but I'd show him if he put me to the test.

I'd gotten there early because I had nothing else to do and, after all that isolation, I couldn't wait to get out of the house. I knew I was ahead of schedule, but upon seeing no one there, a strange unease took over me; maybe it was all a hoax—both the barbecue and Ghiorghis and Libaan's affection. So, just to do something, I began scrambling up a little street bordering the villa. I didn't recognize it, and gradually, while I was climbing, the buildings appeared more and more princely and refined. A construction date was engraved into one of them in roman numerals, MCMXXV, a decisive year for the fascist regime.

When I'd already lost all hope, I finally saw Ghiorghis appear. He was coming up the street, Libaan was next to him, and behind were other friends in their group. When they saw me, they called out: "Little brother, come give us a hand."

They were carrying a big iron grill and some charcoal. The car full of food was parked not far away, but we had to act quickly because it was in a no-parking zone, we needed to unload it and move it. An unbelievable sight: aluminum trays full of shish kebabs stuck out of the trunk—they'd obviously spent the whole day threading meat, bell peppers, and onions; bowls of lettuce, cucumbers, and carrots; fiasco bottles of red wine and two cases of beer.

We moved back and forth between the car and the grill, which we'd set up in a clearing not far away, hidden behind vegetation. When we were done unloading, everyone tried to get involved with lighting the fire.

I pulled out my can, and Ghiorghis said, "Let's see what you can do." So I began the procedure. All around me friends were laughing about how focused I was, while more kids from the old Flaminio crew showed up and Ghiorghis offered everyone wine in paper cups.

I felt very important in front of the fire. I was in the position of control even though it was so hot, the smoke burned my eyes, and I hardly knew anyone. They passed me the skewers, and when I laid them on the grill, they triggered a small flare-up and an intense aroma; afterward we arranged them back in the trays, and everyone took what they wanted. At some point, Ghiorghis called one of his friends over, Jessica, who told me: "Take a break and come help me. Let's bring the beers to the fountain."

The bottles were hot, I held a case against my chest; Jessica wore wooden heels, and her hair looked wet. She walked in front of me wearing a jersey dress, and her shoes went *toc-toc-toc* with each step. The cloth clung to her body, and with each *toc*, her hips swung from one side to the other.

Her shoulders were bare and damp, her long arms lemon-colored, and her big eyes circled with black. A dark depth could be seen in her eyes, like that of a pitch-black well where you can't see the bottom.

I silently watched Jessica, seated on the edge of the fountain, while she stirred the water. She submerged the bottles of beer and said: "This is how we did it in the Flaminio days." She told me other unimportant things, her mouth colored red and her hands delicate—fingers dipping in and out of the fountain.

I fell into Jessica's eyes. All I saw was her mouth opening and closing, I couldn't even understand what she was talking about, maybe I'd had too much to drink. I stared at the red lips while I told her about whatever came to mind, without any precise intent: the phone call, my mother's language, the boarding school, my departure—I spoke without stopping, and the words poured out one after another. Jessica was maybe listening to me, maybe not, and I just wanted to kiss her skin, her shoulders, and she was laughing hard and saying: "Cut it out, you're tickling me," but didn't pull away. She threw her head back, so I kissed her neck, her lemon-colored arms. I took her fingers in my mouth, and the fountain spun, like a merry-go-round, it spun so fast it sprayed everything.

Jessica stirred the water, her jersey dress stuck to her skin, and I rested my head in her lap. She caressed me, wet my hair, smelled it, and said: "Smells like milk and butter."

And I responded, "It's the smell of smoke and wine."

Jessica was born in Cape Verde, like my friend Amilcare, the one from boarding school. She wears shoes with heels, and her hair always looks wet. I don't know how long we stayed at the fountain, she and I. Her chest was small and her dress tight—all her curves could be accurately intuited. I had never been with a woman, and I hardly knew anything about it, even though I'd grown up surrounded by women! My mother, Zia Rosa, and Sissi had taught me many things, but some things they didn't; they couldn't be the ones to teach me those things.

Jessica and I were carrying the cold beers back to the rest of the crew, her heels kept going *toc-toc-toc*, so I asked her: "How are you able to walk in those shoes?"

She told me that when she was a little girl, even back in elementary school, her parents would buy her black shoes with heels because her mother considered them elegant, and she had to wear them even though she hated them. Jessica grew up wearing grown-up shoes, and now she's become so used to them she can't do without hearing a *toc* with each step.

I was entranced by her small feet, her round and muscular legs walking in front of me.

At some point I heard Ghiorghis address me: "Watch out, Jessica loves soap operas. She makes up loads of stories, she's addicted to them." And he winked at us.

Jessica took my hand and brought me to sit off to one side. We both smelled like charcoal, and it seemed to me as though thousands of flaming splinters were orbiting around me. When I told her that the thought of leaving made me sick, she wasn't surprised or saddened, she simply said: "I'm here, I've always lived here. Don't worry, you'll find me here when you return."

They say that many centuries ago at the mouth of the Tiber some fishermen found the statue of a beautiful Madonna caught in their nets. They quickly came back up the river and gifted her to the Trasteverini so that she'd become their guardian. Since then, to commemorate this ancient story, the statue is carried in a procession every summer, along the river and down the streets of Trastevere. Sissi told me she saw her one time and found her enchanting. The Madonna Fiumarola, as they call her, was wearing a beautiful gown adorned with gems, a blue cloak with golden stars, and a crown. She stood all blessed under a canopy among many black cherubs, carried on the shoulders of men in white tunics. As soon as it got dark they set off fireworks. They seemed to light up the entire world.

It makes me think that next time I'd love to see the fireworks from the hospital balcony. While I try to remember when the procession is held, my phone starts ringing. It's an unknown number.

"Yabar, it's me, Sissi." I'm sitting on my bed, the television is on. My roommate is more or less my age, he got here just yesterday for an operation on his teeth. They have to take his wisdom teeth out, it seems they're infected.

"Wait a second," I whisper and slip out into the hallway.

"Mama told me you're in the hospital," she adds. I'm surprised. I thought we'd decided not to tell her.

"We went to London on a field trip, and I wanted to see you, so when I called Mama to ask her for your aunt's number, she had to tell me where you were." I'd thought she was still mad at me. "Remember how you always used to tell me, 'I'll introduce you to my cousins'? I was curious." Sissi laughs uncomfortably. I don't know what to say. "Are you there? Can't you speak?"

"I'm here." My hospital room is the last one on the hallway, right next to the balcony. I go out, I sit down outside. There's a seagull on the roof next door with a red ball in its beak. Who knows what it mistook the ball for, it's so big it could choke him. An old man who had the same idea as I did is out there sipping on a drink, he brought his IV bag with him.

"How did it happen?"

"I didn't want you to know. Don't worry, I'm fine. What did you do in London?"

"We went to the Tate Modern, an art museum. Just think, it used to be a carbon power station. It's on the Thames, on the South Bank. It's so beautiful around there. I really wanted to run along those super-long banks!"

"Are you always thinking about running? You're obviously obsessed!" I say, smiling.

"It's full of street artists: acrobats, jugglers, musicians. Did you go there?"

"Oh, please, the place I saw didn't even seem like London. I was always surrounded by Somalis."

"Must've been great, no?" According to Sissi everything having to do with Somalia is bursting with greatness.

"Well, I guess. A bit intense. What'd you do at the museum?"

“There was this gorgeous Frida Kahlo show. When I’m older, I want to paint like her.”

“Frida who?”

“Remember the Mexican painter? We saw that movie together . . . to make me mad you kept saying they were all just egocentric, decadent artists and that Frida should shave her mustache.”

“Yes, now I remember, but you know I was only joking. No need to get offended . . . the last time we saw each other, you wouldn’t let me into your concert. That hurt, you know? I really wanted to hear your song!”

“I felt hurt too. That’ll teach you how it feels to not be taken seriously. But whatever, it’s no longer important. Mama told me you went back home without telling anyone. What were your cousins like? They didn’t take you around the city at all? They were so boring you wanted to head straight back to Rome?”

How do I explain to her that I was in a neighborhood on the outskirts of London, that we spent most of the time in the house, that they only spoke in Somali, that I never even came close to seeing any English people, that I felt like I was in involuntary exile?

“You know what? My cousins went to Somalia last year,” I say.

“What? How? Isn’t it dangerous?”

“Well, turns out the north is peaceful.”

Maxamed and Muuse, my aunt’s children, had welcomed me with solidarity. They knew what it was like to get into trouble. “Baabuur, car, we took our dad’s car to go joy riding!” And that’s why they had been sent to spend the summer in Somalia. Apparently, it’s true that sending your children away somewhere as punishment is a Somali custom. In the end, I got lucky. London is closer and safer than Gaalkacyo.

“Why wouldn’t you want to go to Somalia?” Sissi asks me.

“My cousins hated it. It was unbearably hot, and there was nothing to do. Muuse, who has braces on his teeth, told me that when he went outside, kids would stare at his mouth, amazed, and yell, 'Diamond, diamond!' as though they were diamonds in his mouth!"

"I don't believe it. This is one of those stories you come up with just to make me laugh!"

That's my little sister. She's on the other end of the phone trying not to laugh. Suddenly, I feel close to her again, as if our fight at the concert had never happened.

"Were you at least able to clear things up about your father?"

"Yes. Now I know what happened, though maybe I'd always known."

15

A FEW YEARS ago, Zia Rosa started an Italian course for foreigners at the library where she works. Mama gives her a hand, and together they've managed to involve a good number of Somali kids who've come over on the boats and escaped death at sea. It engages them on multiple fronts because they don't limit themselves to just planning the lessons. They've set up a genuine volunteer-based reception center: they accompany those in need to the doctor, help them find a place to sleep, put them in touch with someone who deals with the temporary residency permesso procedures and, when necessary, they even provide them with clothing and provisions. Every so often, they entrust me or Sissi with a small task and, as you might expect, my little sister is always over the moon about it.

One Saturday, Mama had invited one of the kids to lunch, and the two of us got to do the shopping. While writing up a list, Mama confessed to us: "The day we left Mogadishu, I couldn't take my eyes off all the children. I had the privilege to save my son, but what would happen to all those who couldn't escape?"

Sissi sighed. "Poor children."

"Know what I think, Sissi?" Mama then added. "It reveals a difference between the sexes. For a woman, an army of children is a tragedy; for a man, it's something he can control."

"You're right!" she replied, all heated. I felt ganged up on, as usual. Why do the men in their conversations always play the role of the idiot?

"Hooyo, what's the boy you invited like? Did he fight too?"

"No, of course not."

"You see, then, that taking up a gun isn't inevitable? It's not like all men go down that road."

"That's not what I was saying, Yabar. I just believe that women are more sensible and feel more compassion. But there are many exceptions, I'll admit. Yasiin, for example, our guest, told me he'd formed a group whose motto was 'Lower the gun, raise the pen.' They wanted to propose an alternative to war. It's a shame that then he began receiving death threats."

Sissi intervened. "Do you think that disarmament could be a solution?"

"Sissi, they've actually tried it a bunch of times, but to hand over their weapons, people have to trust. The problem is they send in international forces who mess everything up. Foreigners aren't the solution," I told her.

"Wait, so you think they should resolve the whole thing on their own?"

"The problem," Mama said while standing up, "is the military." We fell silent. "They pretend to have an ideal of freedom, of fighting against the dictatorship, but they want to make the people believe that the only way to pursue it is by force. They're motivated entirely by greed and seedy economic interests."

"But, Hooyo, but wasn't Papa a—" She shot me a glare. I couldn't finish my sentence.

"A soldier!" Sissi exclaimed. Sometimes her candor really touches me. Mama lets her get away with everything.

"Yes, and it took me a long time to figure it out. Unfortunately, it's in these men's nature"—she paused—"the violence."

"What are we cooking today?" I asked to lighten the mood, but Sissi ignored me.

"Auntie, but the boy who's coming later, could you quickly tell us his story?"

"Yasiin is from Beletweyne. One day, his city was conquered by an adversary clan, so he had to escape. He walked for over fifty kilometers without stopping. Twenty-three hours straight. Seeing as he belonged to the clan that was driven out and he was young, he was afraid they'd kill him. It's what was common practice. When a clan seized power, they took out all the males from the other clan. He arrived at another small city and hid there, but after some days, the clan that had just taken over his city occupied the one he was now in. In what few moments he had to decide whether to go back or continue forward, he heard gunshots. Without thinking twice, he threw himself into the river to cross to the other bank and save himself. He left the little he had behind, even his shoes. Some of the people who weren't as fast and threw themselves into the river behind him were shot dead."

"And then he came straight to Italy?" Sissi loves it when Hooyo loosens up a bit and starts telling stories.

"No, he tried to hold out in Somalia for a few more years. It takes enormous strength to 'enter the journey,' as we say in Somali. And whoever has that strength tries everything possible before leaving. One thing really struck me: when speaking about the civil war, the kids never use the expression 'dagaalka sokeeye,' as if just mentioning it were shameful."

"What do they use instead?"

"Burbur. Which literally means 'shattering.'"

"Did he ever go to Mogadishu?"

"Yes, of course. He went and lived there first, until it became too dangerous. He told me that the city's historic center is now in ruins and that, along with some friends, he toured it—something very risky—to try and imagine how life was before, back when the country was still at peace. They saw the parliament, the government building. You know, that area used to be a labyrinth of narrow streets, a place where at one time many diverse cultures lived side by side—Somali, Arabic, Asian, European—but in the end, it turned into a perfect trap for ambushes and snipers."

"Auntie, it makes me so sad to think that there's no solution, but what do you think—should women rule?"

"That'd be great!"

"What I think is that they need a commander," I said resolutely, and they both looked at me, astonished. "Man or woman, I mean, someone who knows how to take responsibility and who serves the interests of the collective. A person who listens to everyone's side and knows how to distinguish what's right and what's true."

"Well said!" Sissi slapped the table.

"Now quickly go do the shopping," Hooyo urged us. "Our guest will be here in a few hours."

Mom and I spent the day before my departure for London buying gifts. She couldn't send me to our relatives with empty hands, I had to bring something for each member of the family. Naturally, she had received a very complicated wish list—some items specific, some very general, and some no more than vague clues left to her free interpretation.

Being unsure, she chose sweatshirts and T-shirts that read I <3 ROME for her nephews, a pair of leather shoes for her brother-in-law, and some perfume and a Prada bag (fake) for her sister. While paying the Senegalese boy selling her the bag, she had an ironic little grin on her face that I'd never seen before. "She only cares about making an impression, she'll never realize it's not an original." Then she added that it'd been a while since she'd sent so many presents and that Somalis, if someone is coming from Italy, always ask for shoes and bags.

Finally the time came for me to leave. It had been years since I'd taken a plane, I was excited. I'd be able to find a little job in London and buy gifts for everyone, Jessica in particular, even though I'd only just met her. When I thought about her a cold shiver traveled up my spine, it started at my hips and clouded my thoughts, I'd sit in a daze dreaming about her body for hours.

My mother had gotten it into her head that she wanted to accompany me to the airport, so we went to Ostiense Station and took the train to Fiumicino from there: it's fast, it takes only half an hour. Mama was agitated, and excited too—she kept giving me the same advice ("Show respect for the adults," "Watch your big mouth," "Follow the rules," "Don't argue with the boys"), as if she hadn't already told me these things three thousand times before. We'd just checked me in when, while heading toward passport control, she got all anxious that something would go wrong and began asking the security people questions. I was embarrassed because my mom isn't stupid, but that day she was acting like someone who had never in her life taken a plane. By that point, I couldn't wait to leave.

The trip went by fast because I had thoughts of Jessica to keep me company. Once we landed, everything went smoothly, even though there were a bunch of checkpoints because of the attacks and the lines were super long. They took my fingerprints and photo for the British immigration records.

My aunt's husband was waiting for me, he recognized me straight away. Maybe Mama had sent him a photo, or maybe I just hadn't changed much since I was little. "Haye abti, see tahay?" he said.

I felt shy, but was still able to respond with "Waan ficanahay," I'm well, Uncle.

"We go guriga. Everybody, Habaryar, Maxamed, Muuse, tutti, is there!" he said, satisfied with having added in a word in Italian for my sake.

Abti led the way toward his car, a white Ford Escort. He'd decked it out in his own way: a furry steering wheel, a few verses from the Koran hanging on the rearview mirror, there was even a hookah. He works as a taxi driver and spends most of the day in the car. His minicab, as they call the taxis in England that don't have a license from the city, still smelled like roses and smoke—he must've been there waiting for me for quite a while.

"Tutto abbosto? All good? Do you want to watch a movie?" he asked while opening his laptop and pointing at a list of movies.

I replied, "Maya Abti, mahadsanid!" No, thank you, Uncle.

And then he tossed out a satisfied exclamation, "Brafo!" maybe because he'd been worried I only spoke Italian and that we'd ride the whole way in silence. Not that we engaged in very much of a conversation anyway, but just having the ability to speak with me must've reassured him.

They lived in a red brick townhouse, the kind you see all over some parts of London. We parked in the driveway and, the moment she saw the car, Habaryar, my aunt, opened the door to come out to meet us. She seemed to be overflowing with happiness, her eyes tearing up from the emotion. She hugged me, pulling my head onto her shoulder as if I were a child: "Sei grande, so tall!" and, when her husband told her I spoke a bit of Somali, "Waa weynaatay!" she repeated. My aunt looks a lot like Mama, but she's rather short and chubby—I remembered her taller, but so much time had passed. She keeps her hair gathered under a scarf and wears traditional clothing.

Inside the house was the smell of rice and goat. My cousins were sitting in the living room with other people I didn't know. When I walked in, everyone stood up to greet me, and each explained how I was related to them.

"Waxaa dhalay your mother eddadeed wilkeed," he's the son of the son of your mother's aunt. "Waaxaa dhalay your mother awooweheed walaakiis," she's the daughter of the brother of your mother's grandfather. And my head spun with all those possessives, so I just nodded and smiled dazedly.

After the ritual of presentations and welcoming ceremonies, we sat around the long oval table in the dining room, where my aunt had set out many platters: rice, pasta, goat, chicken, salad, and bananas. Meanwhile, my cousins poured a mysterious juice into all the glasses—alcohol isn't drunk during Somali meals, but there's always some syrupy liquid.

There was enough to feed an army, and Habaryar stayed on her feet, she didn't sit with us. That's what Somali women often do—they make sure everyone is doing well and that there's enough food, but they prefer to eat on their own. My mom, instead, values meals together. I bet it's one of reasons why they would tell her she's been Westernized.

"Isbaghetti! Isbaghetti!" my uncle said, pointing at the pasta and laughing, but I preferred the rice, Mama makes it all the time. I took a little with some goat and banana.

Having seen what I chose, Habaryar exclaimed, "Mash'Allah," praise Allah, perhaps because she didn't expect me to know how to combine the traditional foods. And that's how she acted—caught between satisfaction and wonder—for the entirety of the meal. The boys were almost completely silent, the guests chatted, and each time I uttered a word in Somali, whatever it was, even simply *biiyo,* water, Habaryar threw her head back with laughter and told everyone, "Wiilkayga!" My boy, he knows our language! As though they hadn't heard me themselves.

I don't know why she found it so remarkable. I mean, I was still her sister's son and, all things considered, I think I speak Somali pretty badly. It's true my mother had cut ties with everyone, but it doesn't mean she'd forgotten who she was. They clearly didn't understand that.

After dinner, my cousins and I went upstairs to their room, but it was still early, so we started playing *Call of Duty*—the Sybarite's and my favorite shooter video game. The earlier games are set during World War II and seem to be made especially for people obsessed with history like we are. The only thing that bothers me is that the game has already decided who's good and who's bad. One day, I'll write a letter to the creator and remind him that anyone is capable of siding with the winners.

The Sybarite is convinced that good guys and bad guys are always distinguishable: he argues that the Nazis were obviously the bad guys. You can't imagine his shock the day I brought him a documentary on some black South Africans who, since they hated the English, had started using the names of Nazi officials as nicknames! This was, of course, before things went off the rails, before the Afrikaners did what they did.

Well, I couldn't manage to say such complicated things to my cousins, so I settled for playing the part of the American, English, or Russian who fights against the Germans.

About an hour later, Maxamed got a phone call and said, "Let's go to Masaajidka." I stared at him with wide eyes because I wasn't sure I'd understood, but seeing that both he and his brother quickly put the white tunic on over their jeans, the cap and tusbax necklace, I deduced that yes—the mosque was where we were headed. Thankfully, they didn't ask me to put on one of their tunics—that was the last thing I needed. We said goodbye to the adults, who were still chatting in the living room. A car was waiting in front of the house with two boys our age inside, decked out in the same way. My cousins' friend loved driving fast, and a voice reciting the Koran came out of the speakers. From the way he was taking the curves and skidding, it seemed more like we were headed to dance than to pray.

Finally we arrived at the mosque—it was different from how I'd imagined it. The exterior didn't vary much from the surrounding buildings. The mosque was also, in fact, made of red bricks, with a sloping gray roof and a minaret, on top of which was the crescent moon.

"It's time for salaadda," the boys said, which I thought meant, "Let's go pray," or maybe perform ablutions, but since I don't know the prayers and I didn't want to confess this, I pulled out the excuse that I hadn't had the time to take a shower. My mom taught me a few things, far from everything, but I knew that you can't go pee then pray without washing yourself as if it were nothing.

While waiting for them, I observed the men gradually arriving, people of all types and nationalities: old, young, white, black . . . I was reminded of the suicide bomber. I wondered what kind of mosque he'd frequented to become such a fanatic.

As I'd told Ghiorghis, I had tried to be Muslim at various times. When I was little, my father would bring me to the mosque and to Koranic school, and I remember liking it. Over the years, I've attempted to recover his teachings but haven't succeeded. The fact is I was raised by a pragmatic woman who has no particular aptitude for religion, and she trained me to question everything. I was circumcised when I was born "because it's good hygiene," claims my mother, who has never felt compelled to flaunt religious belonging. Mama has always been allergic to extremes ("Whether or not I believe, it's between me and Allah"). She always says that Somalis rediscovered religion as a result of war and exile: they needed to believe in something worth belonging to.

That evening I wanted to learn more about Islamism, so I went to look for my cousins. I found them speaking with a man—he must've been a sheikh—who was showing them a digital Koran in ten languages. I was interested in that Kitaab, so I asked him "Waa meeqa?" How much is it? My cousins were very admiring and, to show me so, bought a prayer mat for me right then and there. It was one with a compass built in so that if you're someone who gets confused with the sun and the cardinal directions, you can never go wrong.

Then, prayers finished and purchases completed, these boys—who had struck me with their faith—diligently folded their tunics once they'd gotten back in the car, took off their caps and tusbax and, putting the car in drive, turned the radio on at full volume and tuned into an entirely different kind of station.

"Let's go to the disco!" Muuse exclaimed, joyfully, and I was so stunned I burst out laughing, thinking they were messing with me—but the boys were completely serious.

The discoteca was full of people, and the boys all ordered something strong. I couldn't believe my eyes: every so often I go overboard with beer, but I rarely drink hard liquor. They'd brought McDonald's cups in with them and immediately transferred what they'd ordered into them. My cousins and their friends didn't want anyone to know that they drank even though everyone was doing it.

Maxamed, who at the beginning had seemed to me a reserved, serious, quiet guy, danced like he was possessed: his knees slightly bent, his pelvis moving back and forth—he even grabbed a dancer around her waist and twirled her as though she were in his own personal music box. It goes without saying that I was terribly embarrassed and slid down in my seat behind a corner of the bar, hoping that no one would come track me down.

That night, when we got home, Habaryar made my cousins swear to Allah that they hadn't had anything to drink and they both replied, "Wallaahi."

That's how I found out that Somali kids who grow up in England are called "say wallaahi" because they're always repeating that word, even when they swear falsely.

16

BEFORE LONG I was brought to the social club. Apparently London is full of the places, frequented primarily by men—the sort of place Mama would hate. My uncle went every day, and as just another male, my presence passed largely unnoticed. The kitchen was open at all hours, there were no women among the cooks nor Western customers among the patrons. They served big portions of traditional food—rice, meat, and spiced tea in abundance. The television was always set to Universal TV, a Somali language channel broadcast in England.

The men discussed universal issues, and the main reason I liked going was that an old man who'd studied in Italy when he was younger was usually there, and every time I walked in he'd make a big deal of it. He couldn't wait to speak in Italian, so he'd invite me to sit at his table: "Are you a big eater? Have a good appetite?" He pronounced the phrases like in the old days and seemed more than happy to buy me lunch. The prices were very economical, and often people who couldn't afford to pay ate on credit. The old man wanted to discuss Italian politics, he overwhelmed me with questions, but he was the one talking most of the time because he read the entire *Corriere della Sera* every day, from start to finish.

My cousins called him Awoowe even though he wasn't actually their grandpa, but because he was higher up in the family tree than their parents and out of respect, among Somalis, you never call an older person by name. Sometimes I'd come with Maxamed, and Awoowe would invite him to lunch too but got all confused with the languages, he'd speak to my cousin in Italian without realizing and, not receiving a reply, would stare at him, taken aback.

Those were the moments that made me want to laugh most: the old man would short-circuit and tell Maxamad: "Prendimi un altro bicchiere di tè!" and my cousin would ask, stunned: "Yaa Awoowe? You are talking in Italian!" and he, to hide his embarrassment, would act as if nothing had happened and ask again for another cup of tea in English or Somali.

Another reason Awoowe amused me was because he had no filter, in the sense that he'd say the first thing that popped into his head. When we first met, for example, the second we were left alone, he asked with a conspiratorial air: "So what can you tell me about your mother?"

I had no idea what kind of information he wanted, but so as not to disappoint him I spit something out: "She's doing well, Awoowe. She works a lot."

"Did she remarry?"

"No, Awoowe."

"Poor thing."

"No, actually, she's happy as is."

"I've always defended her, I've always argued that she's a good girl, but they're all so ignorant!"

"Who, Awoowe?"

"Everyone, everyone!"

When the others joined us, he changed subjects.

That's how I learned from Awoowe that Mama, though resistant to rules (yes, she of all people!), had been considered the family's crown jewel. In fact, my real grandpa (not Awoowe), Allah ha u naxariisto, rest his soul, held her in high regard because she was the only daughter of his to have studied. Awoowe knows that people bad-mouth her, saying, "Waa gaalowday," she's a nonbeliever, she's been westernized, she betrayed her family, but he tells them: "Quit your gossiping, she's a good girl."

This is something I really need to tell Mama, it would make her happy.

In addition to the conversations with Awoowe, two episodes occurred that started making me suspicious.

The first incident took place while I was walking to the social club with my uncle and cousins. We stumbled upon a Somali restaurant that I hadn't noticed before. It seemed identical to the one in our club—the same tables, the same bar, on the same street, even the name was similar: something having to do with the Indian Ocean.

"Why don't we go inta today, go here?" I asked. I thought it would be a good idea to change up clubs for once, I was curious to find out which had better food.

My cousin looked at me as though I were senile: "Yaa? Are you crazy? Kuwii—"

But before he finished his sentence, my uncle gave him a dirty look. "Waryaa, aamus!" Shut up, he told him, and I wasn't quick enough to ask who kuwii were, or rather "those people" who frequented the place.

But the most disturbing episode happened one morning when I was sitting on the couch under the giant picture of my aunt, with lots of makeup and gold filigree jewelry—the types of things Indian women wear. The photo was reflected in the cabinet in front of me, and that's how I noticed a silver frame on the shelf and went closer to look at it. It was a black-and-white photo in which two girls, who could've been my mom and my aunt, hugged a little boy who looked like them both.

I'd never seen my mother when she was younger because she'd gotten rid of all her old photographs, whether out of anger or sadness, I'm not sure. The boy had a beautiful smile.

Driven by curiosity, I dared to take it out of the cabinet and show it to my cousins, who were in the kitchen eating breakfast.

"Who—?" I asked with a whisper, pointing at the girls and little boy. I don't know why I wasn't able to finish my question.

Without even taking his eyes off the cereal box, Maxamed replied that they were our mothers and walaalkood, their younger brother.

"Walaalkood?" I asked, astonished because Mama had never told me about him. I'd thought she and her sister were the youngest siblings.

"Aaway?" Where is he? I added.

And, keeping his gaze down, Maxamed replied: "He died, Allah ha u naxariisto."

I wanted to know more, but trying to get answers out of him was like pulling teeth. How and when did our mothers' brother die? Why had no one ever told me?

"Omicidio killed him. Don't you know what Omicidio did?" Muuse said, who up until that moment hadn't made a sound.

While asking him, "Do you know what Omicidio means?" my aunt walked into the kitchen and silence fell.

I showed the photo to her, asking her about the little brother Mama had never mentioned to me, and Habaryar said she wasn't surprised that Mama had never mentioned him. She said it coldly and added: "Our civil war killed him when he was only twenty."

At that moment, all the words I'd overheard as a boy, whenever Mama turned up the volume of the music, rushed back to me. I had thousands of questions to ask, but all the lips in that house were sealed. I went out to look for the old man, he wouldn't be so reticent, or at least he wouldn't hide behind the weak excuse of language.

I found him sitting with some men, all sipping tea and, since I looked upset, he asked me: "What's wrong?"

"Awoowe, I have to talk to you about something important. Alone." I told him.

The old man excused himself from his comrades, and we sat down a short distance away. I had one hand palm down on the table and a lighter in the other, which I handled like a knife, bouncing it between my fingers, it went *tum* each time it hit the table. Awoowe put his hands over mine, saying: "Don't shake that or it will blow up in your hands."

In a pleading tone of voice, I asked him to explain why everyone was keeping the truth hidden from me, every truth: Who were the people that went to the other club? Why was my mother's younger brother dead? And, above all, who had committed a homicide?

Awoowe cleared his throat—I was giving him a great responsibility, and he needed to speak in the most transparent way possible.

"Your mother must have told you that unimaginable violence was committed during the war in the name of the clan: members of the same family fought against each other, killed one another in cruel ways. This was what Afweyne, Bocca Grande, the dictator, left us as his legacy: discord and destruction. Clans aren't the cause in and of themselves—power and greed are what guide men's actions—but clans did provide pretext. Then, as if the situation weren't dramatic enough already, foreign contingents intervened by backing one leader and unseating another, all with the illusion of restoring peace and the desire to manipulate Somali politics. Things could only get worse . . . no one—Somali or foreigner—cared about making decisions for the good of the people, they only wanted to seize as much as possible for personal gains."

"Yes, but who are kuwii?"

Awoowe grabbed my hands again and said: "The people from the other club aren't enemies, they're simply other Somalis, linked to you on your father's side, while I, and your aunts and uncles, are relatives of your mother's father."

Then why couldn't we go in there if they were simply other Somalis? Maybe if I'd only asked, they would've helped me figure out what had happened to my father. Why had Aabbe, if he truly loved me, stopped looking for me?

"This is how we Somalis are, you just have to accept it," the old man told me. "Children must be the ones to look for their fathers. They belong to the women until they become adults."

And why had Mama kept me away from her family? What had happened to her brother?

The music on Universal TV was too loud, and a horrible noise filled my ears. My temples pulsated from all the tension. I asked the old man: "Can't they turn it down?" and while the words came out, I thought of my mom turning up the music so she wouldn't be heard.

Awoowe went and asked them to lower the volume. He seemed relieved, he needed a break. He came back a few minutes later with two more cups of tea.

"Yabar, the problem is that until we Somalis acknowledge what we did to one another, until the guilty admit to their own responsibilities in the massacre, there's no hope for our country."

I no longer remembered my father's face, the only photo I had of him I kept in my wallet. It was the frightening collage where one of his eyes is bigger than the other, his mouth is on his neck, and his forehead is too low.

I pulled it out and slid it across the table: "Did you know him?" I asked and burst into tears. I don't know why, it'd been years since I'd cried.

Everyone was looking at me, and the old man whispered: "Come now, keep your chin up. Don't cry. You're an adult now." He grabbed me by the arm and led me outside, distancing me from his friends' curiosity.

"Awoowe, I have to smoke, I'm sorry," I said and lit a cigarette while, as much as I tried to stop, the tears kept streaming down.

He invited me to walk with him to calm myself down a bit, and we arrived in front of the other club. I stopped to peek in through the window.

"Stop acting like a spy," he scolded me. "That's rude."

I kept my hand deep in my pocket, and with my fingers I felt the pointy corners of the photo of my father, they tickled my fingertips and gave me courage: "Maybe Omicidio wasn't the one who killed my mother's younger brother, maybe his militia did it accidentally."

The old man smiled, and I saw the dark roots of his teeth.

"It doesn't make any difference, nobody really cares. Maybe your mother's younger brother was armed and Omicidio murdered him or had him murdered by one of his people, or maybe not. Your mother's younger brother wasn't part of the same clan as Omicidio: that's the most important thing, and it's why he was killed. There's no other reason."

I felt myself suffocating. I still heard music in my ears, but this time it didn't muffle any ugly words—it amplified them instead: The dogs still hadn't had enough, they wanted to keep killing, and my mother had sent me to boarding school to hide me from evil, so no one would infect me with the hate and I would never know what Omicidio had done.

But my father commanded an army, it couldn't be hard for him to find a little boy hidden at a boarding school. So he came to visit me, making me the happiest kid in the world.

We were still in front of the other club's entrance. I told the old man: "I know my father is Omicidio, but I'd hoped he was a hero." And, because I was on the verge of sobbing convulsively, I took off. I ran faster than Sissi, faster than the river. The wind picked up the leaves, and I felt as vulnerable as a swallow.

Before boarding school, my parents and I lived together in Rome and my father came and went, sometimes dressed for war, sometimes dressed for peace, and his wife loved him very much. I imagine she loved him up until her younger brother was murdered and my father was nicknamed Omicidio.

My mother kept the music loud. Her brother was killed at the hand of Omicidio or on his orders, and she didn't want me to know the whole story, and yet I've always known it. It's just that I'd realized I no longer knew I'd known it.

It's my fourth day in the hospital when my mom finally comes. She took her time, that's for sure; still, it does take a while to get home from way up there where she was. At the very instant in which she crosses the hospital threshold, I feel something like an air pressure shift, lighting and thunder on their way. She calls my phone.

"Where are you, Yabar? I've already gone up and down the stairs at least three times!" Maybe I'd only been in the bathroom, but when Mama is distressed, she loses her sense of direction. I'm used to it by now. I go meet her in the stairwell. I must not look that great because when she sees me she bursts into tears.

"You've gotten so skinny," she says. She's already lost the firm tone of voice from a few minutes ago. There's a cold mango juice in her bag and pistachio sweets. I do the honors. Mama remarks, like everyone does, that this hospital is better than she'd expected.

"Rosa brought me up to date, tomorrow I'll be the one to accompany you to your appointment."

"Have you spoken to your sister?" I ask. I want to control the conversation for once. It won't likely happen again.

I think I've only succeeded on one occasion, a couple of years ago, thanks to Zia Rosa and Sissi's support. We were talking about Somalia, just for a change, and Mama was giving us a history lesson.

A transitional Somali government had just been formed, and we'd heard that the appointments would be distributed in accordance with the so-called Cencelli Handbook.

"Which does not mean—mind you—that the posts will be assigned based on political belief, but rather on clan affiliation," Zia Rosa pointed out.

"What does clan mean?" Sissi asked. "Is that who fought against one another during the war?"

Mama threw a dirty look at Zia Rosa, who'd introduced the topic. "I don't want to talk about such things."

"Mama, you have to explain it to Sissi, otherwise she'll be confused and nothing will make any sense," I begged her, turning then to Sissi with the air of someone in the know. "For her it's taboo."

"It's true, it's taboo for various reasons, but the main one is that clannism is our misfortune and naming the affiliations only serves to reaffirm their importance. Somalis didn't kill one another in the name of their clans, but by means of their clans."

"But it still needs to be talked about, Zahra, if we want to move past it. The kids need to understand."

"And you want me to teach them these divisions?" she lashed out. "Speaking about it only causes pain, it won't do any good."

Meanwhile, Sissi had taken a book down from the shelf, and she opened it to a sort of family tree on one of the first pages.

"Look, here are all the names of the clans and the relationships between them."

"You see?" Zia Rosa intervened. "It'd be better if you were the one to describe the situation, otherwise they'll get the wrong idea."

"All Somalis are Muslim, they all look the same, and they speak only one language, right?" Sissi then pressed her.

"Exactly. The one thing you two have to learn is that the clan is only an instrument of power, just as all divisions are, after all. But it doesn't represent political belief—you belong to a clan by birth and never by choice."

"That's right! Did you know, Sissi, that my parents are from two different clans?" I added, my mother glaring at me.

Mama takes a little break to calm herself, she pours the fruit juice into two plastic cups but doesn't answer me when I ask about her sister.

"Can you at least tell me how you were able to get married, you and my father, even though you didn't belong to the same clan?"

"There wasn't all this hate back then. It was different. Or we were, at least."

"But you yourself told me that in order to get married you had to ask for permission."

"You don't understand. We didn't ask for permission. The elders were the ones who had to reach an agreement."

All her lectures about modernity, and then I'm the one who doesn't understand that to get married you need to have your elders' consent!

"But wait—in Italy, it's enough for the couple to want it. What are you saying?"

"It's complicated. I chose your father, it wasn't an arranged marriage. We went out together at night, we were dating, and there were no problems with that. But marriage is another thing altogether, the fathers make the decision. In the past, it was also a way to form alliances."

"Yeah, in the Middle Ages."

"Quit it, Yabar. We belonged to two different clans, our fathers' decision wasn't enough. In the end, the elders had to go before the sheikh, the religious leader."

"Along with my father, of course. Where were you, Mama?"

"With the women. They got me ready, I was the bride. You know how I am, I would have preferred to get married in a simple way. It was very difficult for me. I wore gold jewelry, the most beautiful clothes. In the end, we aren't alone in the world. We must accept the rules even if they don't sit right with us. It's like I always tell you."

"But at some point you stopped following the rules." And with that, I take an old photo out of my backpack with her as an adolescent hugging her sister and little brother.

My mother falls silent, she swallows a sweet whole without chewing it first. She stands up as if to leave, but can't manage to take a step forward. She clings to a chair. I go to her, she could collapse at any moment.

"Okay. I'll tell you what really happened," she says.

"Take a seat." I motion toward the chair. Best to take advantage of the opportunity, never mind that sometimes she behaves irrationally. She clears her throat and looks me directly in the eye.

This time she has to tell me the story from start to finish.

17

I'D BEEN IN London for a week already, but I still hadn't seen any of the city. I could have been anywhere—England, Australia, Minnesota—but it felt like I was in Somalia: the shopkeepers were almost all Sikh or Bangladeshi, but there were also call centers, Money Transfers, and restaurants run by Somalis, not to mention the people all around the neighborhood. Veiled women, children of all ages dragged by hand or pushed in a stroller, teenagers, old people—and everyone said hello to one another like in a small town.

One time I saw Awoowe reprimand some kids shoving one another on the sidewalk. I first thought he knew them, but instead it was just because they were Somali that he assumed the right to yell at them. The first few days, also, I was very surprised to see that girls wore the veil, I wasn't used to it.

While running away from the club in tears, I felt everyone's eyes on me: no one runs like a maniac through a small town. People stared at me, confused, so I gradually slowed my pace until I was walking like everything was normal, though I was still crying. The Omicidio story disturbed me, but what upset me more was the rage I felt toward my mother.

She could have just told me what had happened, there was no need to send me off on my own to find out the truth. It was her fault I'd made a fool of myself in front of my aunt and cousins, not to mention all the crying at the club.

I needed to hurl these thoughts at her right away, so I stopped in a call center to call her. Naturally, her first reaction was to say it was my fault: me and my emotions. I wasn't there to get mixed up in old stories that had nothing to do with me. I could've signed up for an English course and looked for a job instead of wasting time with the old people in the club.

As if it were an everyday occurrence to discover that your father, who you haven't heard from in a while, is in reality an assassin!

"This just shows that I made the right choice!"

"To keep me away from the Somali community? Hide me from my father?"

"Exactly. You're not the first or the last kid to grow up without a father . . . instead you have to thank heaven you have a mother like me!"

"Do you want to tell me why you sent me to the Somalis in London?" It was contradictory and incomprehensible, to first distance me from an environment and then throw me back into it. What was she trying to do?

Mama went ballistic: "To teach you a lesson." And she hung up without leaving me time to respond.

I was out of my mind. An entire month in that place added up to a cruel punishment. I had no desire to hear every goddamn day that my father had murdered my uncle. I was still inside the call center booth so, to calm myself down, I decided to call Jessica.

"What are you doing still there? Change your ticket and come back to me." Her voice was beautiful and so soothing it immediately helped me overcome the anguish.

I felt, though, that I had to face the issue head on. I had to go to the other club and ask for news of my father. Hopefully someone knew him and could tell me where he'd ended up.

Back at the house, I didn't speak to anyone about my conversation with Awoowe, and my cousins were very careful not to bring up anything about the homicide. I didn't sleep a wink all night, and at dawn, I got up with the purpose of going in search of information. I knew my father's full name, that should be enough: Mama always says that Somalis all know one another because there aren't many of us and everyone has a prodigious memory. Through family relationships we're able to trace back to anyone's identity.

As I got closer to the club, however, I began losing my conviction and my anxiety grew. Once I arrived, I peeked inside, as I'd done the previous day when I was there with Awoowe.

At that very moment, a man came out and, after looking me up and down, said: "The old man isn't with you today, eh, Yabar?" He walked away chuckling.

Hearing him utter my name, I felt a pang in my heart. How did he know who I was? Had the community been informed that Omicidio's son was in town?

I knew that Somalis know everything about everybody, but I never imagined the full extent. Maybe it would be better to let it go and return to Rome, to Jessica, before getting into any trouble. So instead I slipped into a travel agency without overthinking it and, paying a fee, I managed to change my return flight. I decided that I'd leave in a few days, the time needed to study the route to the airport while keeping my intentions secret. If I had said I wanted to leave, my aunt would've found a way to stop me.

I spent the next couple of days concentrating on my escape plan. So as to not arouse suspicion, I had my cousins bring me to a local temp agency and I pretended to look for a job.

Again, to keep a low profile, with the excuse of going to enroll at an English language school, I left the house the morning of my departure with only my small backpack. Inside, I'd stealthily stuck the photo of Mama's younger brother. I was way ahead of schedule, but shook with anxiety nonetheless, worried that the buses would get stuck or that someone would discover me before I boarded.

Everything seemed to be going according to plan until, upon walking into the airport, I was confronted with endless security lines. I panicked—if I had to wait in line I would never make it through in time. They'd increased security following the bombing attempts. Fortunately, it was all carefully thought out, such that every fifteen minutes a security agent passed by to call for the passengers whose boarding time was imminent so that no one would miss their flight.

Finally, to my great relief, the plane took off. It was done; I could no longer be stopped. The trip lasted less than three hours, but it'd been days since I'd slept, so I had the sensation that we were in the air forever. Right when the plane landed, I rushed toward the door, as though my fate would change if I were the first to get off.

When you travel to London and back, you have to go through passport control, and usually when you're in the line reserved for European citizens, they don't stop you; however, that day the officer had woken up on the wrong side of the bed.

"And this guy in the photo, is that you?" he asked me, laying his Roman accent on thick, maybe to see if I could still understand him.

"Yeah, who else would it be?" I responded in the same tone of voice.

Admittedly, I'd gotten my passport a few years earlier and my face had been a bit rounder back then. Come to think of it, I looked like my mother's younger brother—I wonder if he'd been my age when they took the photo.

The guy called other officers over, and I got even more nervous because I was in a rush to get to Jessica. I grumbled to myself, "The usual racists!"—that's what I thought, no point in denying it. I could tattoo my Italian passport on my chest, and it still wouldn't stop them from tearing me to pieces—tossing language to one side, hands and eyes to another.

Hearing the word "racists," the officers started getting worked up, and one of them, maybe the oldest, maybe the highest ranking, goes: "Hey kid, simmer down—you know who I am?"

And I don't know what came over me, sometimes phrases slip out on their own. I replied: "Who might you be, the mayor of Duckburg?"

The guy lost it and ordered the pigs to bring me to the police station. While we were walking there, they wouldn't stop provoking me—about how skinny I was, who did I think I was, and so forth. It was just a game for them really, but I kept falling for it and calling them snakes, losers, fascists, which naturally did nothing but make the situation worse.

Then the boss, or rather the mayor of Duckburg, after having checked my background information again and still coming up with nothing to grasp at, ordered me to get down on the floor and do fifty push-ups: "This way you'll get a good start to your visit and you'll learn to keep calm next time."

I was sweating, and his henchmen were laughing at me: "You're skinny but strong, eh, boy?" And I was so full of rage that I could feel it explode under my hands.

In the end they let me go with the expectation that I'd learned a lesson, but I didn't want to learn a damn thing—at that moment all I cared about was rushing to Jessica's and spending the night with her. I put my passport back in my pocket with the photos of my father and of my mother's little brother, and I went to take the train that goes to Tiburtina, not far from Jessica's house.

Once I reached the station, I began walking toward Portonaccio because I didn't feel like waiting for the bus, and continued until I reached her house. My heart was pounding, no one knew where I was at that moment. I felt like the freest man on the face of the planet.

I found Jessica, all happy, waiting for me on the sidewalk. To get to her building you need to go through a sort of tunnel and, because the street numbers are hard to see, she was worried I'd get lost. It was a bit dark down there, gray walls and abandoned stores—I wondered whether she felt scared whenever she got home late. Her steps echoed in the tunnel just like the day I'd met her, and I felt a sort of heat fill me. The sound of her heels was her signature.

Jessica shared the house with two other girls, but at that moment they were both on vacation, so she had me sit down in the kitchen: "You must be hungry," she said. "It's almost dinnertime."

There was some sad music playing in the background. Jessica told me it was a morna, a traditional dance from Cape Verde. She showed me the steps, squeezing me tight, and I wanted to collapse because it was my first time dancing with a woman. The song was called "Sodade," which essentially means "nostalgia," even though Jessica said that for Capeverdians it's a bit different. They're melancholic people—their country is, in fact, a small archipelago in the middle of the Atlantic, and whoever is born there believes they'll never manage to leave, and when they leave, they believe they'll never be able to return.

The music kept playing, and meanwhile Jessica opened the freezer and asked me: "Do you like french fries and meatballs?" I nodded, and so she set to work: she combined ground meat, egg, milk-soaked bread, salt, and mixed it all together with her hands to then make many meatballs using her fingertips. Watching her, I thought she looked like the sexiest woman on the planet: Jessica wore her wooden heels in the house as well, and a very short dress made of lightweight jersey, just as she liked them.

The menu sounded great to me. My mother and Zia Rosa never made frozen french fries. When Sissi and I were little, they always told us: "Fried and frozen foods are carcinogenic," and they say the same still today. I think there are many cancer-causing things in the world, and I've also always loved french fries.

Jessica poured a bottle of sunflower oil into the fryer, and when it got hot, she put the entire basket of frozen french fries in it. The whole kitchen smelled like fried food, and she kept laughing in delight and hugging me: "You came back early, I'm so happy!"

In that moment, I felt like I wanted to spend my life with her, like I'd wanted with Stella Ricorsi, to do things together every day, wake up next to each other every morning. After eating we moved to her bedroom. It was full of frills—the bed had a lace cover, and there was a porcelain cherub on the bedside table. Her makeup and perfumes were lined up neatly on the dresser.

We sat down, and Jessica took my hands and put them between her round and muscular legs. She arched back, squeezing me with her calves. Her stomach and mouth smelled like butter and charcoal, and I wanted to go into that mouth and that stomach.

I don't know what it was, maybe the sound of her heels falling to the floor, but all of a sudden, the story of the old lady shoes that she'd told me the evening we met came to mind and, no matter what I did, I couldn't get it out of my head. There was a big mirror with a gold frame in front of the bed where you could see our entangled bodies reflected. We looked like a single creature with four arms and four legs.

I'd never been with a woman, and that mirror seemed to be tearing me to pieces and mixing everything up. I saw parts of my body and my face spinning like in a blender, and they transformed into pieces of Omicidio, the suicide bomber, and my mother's brother.

I told Jessica: "I look at myself in the mirror, and my face and body look so different." I tried to explain so many things to her, but she couldn't understand them—maybe she was still thinking about her black heels.

She no longer knew how to distract me, and so, perhaps in an attempt to make me laugh, she put her hands together and began singing a nursery rhyme she'd learned as a child: "*Toc toc.* Quem é? Sou eu, Dona Eugênia. Olá. Como está? Tudo bem? *Smack smack.* Tudo bem? *Smack, smack.*" Her fingertips touched each other, thumb to thumb, pointer to pointer, pinky to pinky, and back in the other direction. In the end, the two middle fingers gave each other a kiss.

With each repetition Jessica laughed, and I felt even more embarrassed. Her body smelled like butter and charcoal, and in the mirror I saw the reflections of many faces, many bodies, but face and body were ours alone.

I quickly got dressed while Jessica tried to keep me from leaving: "What are you doing? It's late!" But I didn't feel like responding to her or listening to her, she only made me feel worse. I just wanted to get downstairs and outside as fast as possible.

Jessica kept saying: "Where are you going? These things happen, you don't need to feel ashamed." But I had never been with a woman, and thanks to a mirror and a pair of shoes with heels, I have still never been with a woman.

18

WHEN THE RIVER meets the sea, the waters mix together. The seagulls follow it to its mouth and go back and forth on the beach; they come up against the undertow and line up to wait. Before the start of summer, a machine comes through to level the sand, making it compact and erasing traces of passersby. A clean, clear path emerges where footprints don't blend but remain visible to all.

Today they're going to do an ocular ultrasound, Mama and I are sitting in the waiting room. Doctor Bandanna has just come in, he waves hello. There are two other doctors with him—the mean colleague from the first day and a female doctor. The woman has a black bob and a polka-dotted skirt that reminds me of Stella Ricorsi's—I wonder if Stella will look like her when she grows up. Maybe I'll call her when I get out of here, I want to tell her I'm sorry.

Mama sits next to me, she pulls a book out of her bag and starts reading.

"What book is that?" I ask. It seems strange that she's able to concentrate at a moment like this.

"*The Moon and the Bonfires* by Cesare Pavese," she replies, her eyes glued to the pages, as though nothing else exists.

Finally it's my turn. The doctor shakes my mom's hand: "He gave you quite the surprise, eh?" She gets the hint that she's not allowed to come in with me. Once I'm inside, everything happens quickly. They take the gauze off again, it's the same ophthalmoscope as the first day, and the doctors crowd around the screen, speaking in serious tones.

At some point, Doctor Bandanna exclaims, "Yes!" a bit like someone yelling out "goal" in front of a soccer match on TV.

"Good news?" I ask, somewhat timidly.

"The hematoma is reabsorbing well," he explains.

"Don't get too excited, it's still early," his colleague (the one who likes to scare me) is quick to add. The other doctor says nothing. Then we do another vision check with the light box chart. I'm healing, thank God.

"It's a miracle," they say more than once.

Mama stands up as soon as she sees me walk out. I smile, she hugs me. "I hoped that seeing you would help them forgive me," she says. "I was missing my family, Yabar, I never expected you'd experience so much pain and suffering."

Three allied armies marched toward the capital—from the north, the south, and the interior. Along their long advance, they passed through villages, cities, encampments, and the people clapped because their mission was to dethrone Afweyne, Bocca Grande, the cruel dictator. As they came closer to the center of power, the commanders could taste their victory, and seeing as they had neither food nor wealth to soften up the soldiers, they promised them carte blanche, a free pass. "After a hundred years of tyranny, you'll finally have your share of the loot."

In reality, each commander secretly cultivated the desire to become the new undisputed leader, the tyrant's substitute. No one in the city was aware of the wrongdoing the armies were about to carry out and, when they arrived victorious, the people welcomed them with great rejoicing. Many had trusted their promises; they didn't know the soldiers were trained to kill and that before long they'd be violating houses, women, children.

Even Mama had believed it all, she'd hoped they were sincere, but what she wanted most was to save my father—she was afraid he'd die. He'd been in the military during peacetime, what did he know about fighting? She convinced him, and they left together for Rome as soon as they sensed the first hints of danger: Mama had been right. Soon thereafter, the city would be torn apart by the fighting. The people were divided into those who joined the soldiers and those who fled in terror—by foot, in cars, any way they could, even in carts pulled by donkeys.

In Italy, my father suffered. "You kept me from participating in the liberation of our people," he'd yell at my mother, and she'd respond saying war isn't the solution, it never has been. He didn't listen: he came and went from Somalia, he made alliances, planned attacks, and Mama no longer trusted him. "Soon we can return to a country at peace," he promised, and when she asked about the massacres, he reassured her: "It's all propaganda."

When the war broke out in Mogadishu, my maternal grandparents moved to a little city toward the south and stayed there for a couple years, seeking refuge in the villages, just scraping by like fugitives. Grandpa decided not to flee the country, and my mother's younger brother was very close to him—he didn't want to abandon him. One day he called my mother. It was 1992. The great foreign powers were about to intervene, bringing new imbalances and resources to distribute.

He begged her to convince their father to flee the country. Soon there would be a bloodbath, the warlords controlled the city, and they were determined to destroy every obstacle standing in the way of their absolute power. Quite a few important people, including my grandpa, were blacklisted just because of their affiliation. My mother didn't believe her brother, she told him that clans were an illusion and propaganda and that if things got ugly, my father would undoubtably save them.

At the time, in fact, he wasn't far from where they were, and she begged her brother to get in touch, to ask his help in fleeing the country. She gave him the directions to the place where my father, with the army he commanded, had established his general headquarters. My mother's brother trusted his sister; he went and never came back. Word later got out that he'd been killed on the spot. My grandparents awaited the return of their son in vain, and eventually, once they were certain he'd never return, decided to leave Somalia, overcome with grief. They fled by sea and later settled in Kenya, in Nairobi. My grandpa never forgave my mother for having sent his son to die.

That evening, after leaving Jessica's house, I set off at a good pace. I didn't have any real destination, and I had to blow off some steam. The last thing I needed was yet another failure. I'd dreamed of Jessica's mouth and stomach for days, I'd desired her so strongly, and yet in the hours I'd spent with her I couldn't manage to do anything. In the mirror facing the bed I'd seen myself transfigured: Omicidio's mouth, the suicide bomber's hands, my mother's brother's eyes . . . like a bomb that explodes, scattering and mixing up the pieces of various bodies.

I covered the length of Via Tiburtina, all the way to the university, and then I lost my bearings—it's an area I hardly know. Thankfully there were some people around, so I took the opportunity to buy a couple beers and ask for directions to Termini Station.

It must've been around midnight when I left the station behind me and started down Via Nazionale. While walking along with great strides, I gulped down a beer as if it were water and stopped from time to time to have a cigarette. All I had with me was my little half-empty backpack—I'd left some things in London, some at Jessica's house, and at one point my head was flooded with strange thoughts—I wondered how heavy the bag carrying the African women's food, the bag the homeless woman gave me as a present, and the one full of the bomber's explosives all might have been. I saw them rolling one after the other down the street; they dodged the cars and passersby and spilled their contents out on the asphalt.

I hadn't slept for three nights, and all around me resounded a multitude of nursery rhymes, all incomprehensible, made up of incoherent sounds—the problem is that inside one's own head it's impossible to turn the volume down.

I arrived in Piazza Venezia, and the Vittoriano was in its usual place, white and imposing like a temple. There's a bar on the corner of Via del Corso, open round the clock. I didn't know where to go, so I ordered another beer and just stood for a while in the middle of the piazza, feeling sorry for myself. My father was an assassin, I was impotent, all the people I loved had bailed on me—what more could I expect from life?

Then I got an idea. The river was nearby, I only had to cross the Garibaldi Bridge and I'd be at Cantiere. Where had all my bad luck begun if not at that centro sociale? Maybe I could formulate a spell and start all over again: I'd be dating Stella Ricorsi, and I would've gone to the Queen of the Giants concert accompanied by Sam and His Pietrini.

While ruminating—by then drunk—on how great it would be to go back in time, I started walking, and after only fifteen minutes, I was there.

There were quite a few people outside, all in line to get in. My head was spinning, I was tired, and the beer had me in a daze. Everything seemed strange and slow. I didn't know what to do, so I got in line as well. In front of me was a group of friends and, seeing that I was alone, one of them asked me: "Hey, brother, you're here for the concert too?"

Unlike Ghiorghis and his comrades, these kids didn't have black hands like mine, and when I replied, "Why are you calling me brother when you don't even know me?" the guy didn't burst out laughing.

Instead he took offense and responded: "You came here for the concert like we did, that's why I called you brother."

The musicians were rehearsing, you could hear the melodies of the songs, and the kids tried to convince me that reggae turns all people fighting against oppression into brothers and sisters.

Those kids thought that calling me brother was enough to make me feel welcome, but none of them could understand the story of Omicidio or that of the bomber; they couldn't understand the story of Sissi, Zia Rosa, my mother, the Sybarite, Stella Ricorsi, Ghiorghis, Libaan, and Jessica; ultimately, none of them could understand the first thing about me.

The voices reached me distorted, and I understood that I'd never find my friends at that place again and that it wasn't where I wanted to be. So, while walking away, I lifted my arm to say goodbye: "Heil! Heil! To all of you!"

They stared at me with eyes wide, like they were looking at a crazy person. "What's the matter with you?" one of them asked. And as I kept going, "Heil! Heil!" and laughing hysterically and convulsively, various voices could be heard from the line: "Who is he?" "Is he drunk?" "What'd you drink?" But none of them dared challenge me, because that word can be taboo for others, but it can't be for me.

After having turned the corner, I collapsed to the ground and was taken by the incontrollable urge to vomit, and Jessica's dinner spilled out onto the sidewalk. I tried to pick myself up to cross over. I could hardly stand, and I threw myself into the middle of the street without even looking. Out of the corner of my eye, I saw a motorcycle racing toward me at full speed. I attempted get out of the way, but it was too late and *bang*!—no more sounds, only silence.

The rearview mirror nailed my cheekbone, the motorcyclist skidded across the asphalt, raising up a cloud of sparks, and an oncoming car was unable to avoid him.

I don't know how badly he was hurt, I didn't see him stand back up. I stayed in the dark, leaning against a tree—I was too scared and stunned to help. That's how I discovered that when you've been hit hard, your brain prevents you from feeling any pain.

Fatebenefratelli Hospital is nearby, I told myself. I can get there on my own. If need be I'll have them give me stitches, and then I'll go home. I wasn't even thinking about my eye, I only felt guilty about the motorcyclist. Who knows how badly he'd been hurt because of me? Thankfully the ambulance came right away—I heard it—and in the following days the local news didn't refer to any serious accidents.

Sissi came straight from the airport, she didn't even stop at home first. Her entrance into the hospital seems scripted, my little sister never goes unnoticed. "Ladies and gentlemen, behold the queen of the giants in the flesh!" She comes out onto the balcony with her blond hair even bigger than before, wearing a colored scarf around her neck. Everyone, patients and visitors, turn to look at her.

"Yabar!" She doesn't even give me the time to stand up, she hugs me while I'm still seated.

"You didn't need to rush, you know I'm stuck here."

"I couldn't wait to see you." Sissi likes to act tough, but she's too sentimental to pull it off fully.

"So?" She sits down next to me. "I heard there's some good news!"

"Yes, Doctor Bandanna is pleased."

"Doctor Bandanna?"

"My eye doctor."

"Is that actually his name, or is it your nickname for him?"

"What do you think?" I'd forgotten how easy it was to make her laugh.

"How do you come up with such things?"

"Well . . . in this case it didn't take much imagination. Anyway, the doctor says that if I keep it up I'll recover even more."

"So your eye will return to normal?"

"It's likely that part of the damage will be for life, but I won't be blind forever!" Sissi squeezes my hand. "Don't be sad, it could've gone thousands of times worse."

"When did you get so wise?"

What a strange feeling, it's my eye that won't return to normal, yet I feel strong enough to console Sissi. "And then who knows, with all the scientific research happening in medicine they're making such steady progress, maybe in a few years they'll discover a remedy."

"Let's hope so."

"Now tell me about you—did you have fun?"

"When will they discharge you?"

"In a few days, I think."

"It doesn't make sense to talk about me; you instead . . ."

"I have so much to tell you. A bunch of stories. I don't even know where to start."

"From the end."

"There isn't an end."

"At least tell me why you left London without warning anyone. What happened that was so horrible?"

"Nothing in particular, I was just angry."

"At whom?"

"Remember when we argued? I said something terrible."

"Yes, that I couldn't understand you because I'm white. Don't remind me."

"Now I know I was wrong. And I want to say I'm sorry."

"I'm glad you're apologizing, but what happened that was so illuminating it made you change your mind?"

"Nothing, it's just that a person's story is much more complex than the color of their skin. Each of us has something different inside . . . eyes alone aren't enough to see, they stop at appearances, they can't go deeper."

"I can tell that the hospital has definitively cracked your sound, racist principles!"

"I'm being serious, you know."

"I know, this time I'm the one joking. Now, tell me about your father."

"Maybe I could find him, Mama says it wouldn't be too hard."

"How?"

"She says I just have to ask the right people . . . Anyway, you asked why I came back, and to be honest, I think I have the answer . . . when I was in London, I understood that I didn't actually care one bit about finding out where my father was. Deep down I don't even know who he is. You're my family, Sissi—you, Mama, Zia Rosa—and Rome is our home."

Sissi is moved, she hides her face behind her scarf.

"Let's go outside," I say. "I want to see the river."

"You think they'll let you out?"

"We'll come right back, I'm sure they won't even notice."

We go down the stairs undetected. We sneak through a service door next to the bar that no one was guarding. The Tiber's a few steps away. There's something solemn about looking out over the river again—we don't even feel like speaking loudly, only at a whisper. I see some tree trunks on the water's surface, like the backs of crocodiles. Crocodiles are a necessary evil, and to govern over them, one needs great determination. The commander of the river is capable of distinguishing good from evil, he recognizes their essences. He doesn't betray the people's trust, he doesn't abandon his family, he doesn't kill innocent people. Finally, after so many years, I understand. It's not my father; it's me, Yabar—I'm the commander of the river.

Ubah Cristina Ali Farah, a poet, novelist, playwright, librettist, and oral performer, was born in Verona, Italy, of a Somali father and an Italian mother. Raised in Mogadishu, she fled at the outbreak of the civil war at the age of eighteen. Her publications include stories, poems, and three novels, including *Little Mother* (Indiana University Press, 2011) and *The Stations of the Moon* (66thand2nd, 2021). Ali Farah holds a PhD in African Studies from Naples's Università L'Orientale. She has received Lingua Madre and Vittorini Prizes and has participated in many residencies and writing programs around the world.

Hope Campbell Gustafson has an MFA in Literary Translation from University of Iowa and a BA from Wesleyan University. Her work can be found in various journals, *Banthology: Stories from Unwanted Nations,* and *Islands—New Islands: A Vagabond Guide to Rome* by Marco Lodoli. From Minneapolis, now living in Brooklyn, Campbell Gustafson is Senior Program Associate for the Civitella Ranieri Foundation.